MW00979273

BEWHISKERED TALES

Boomish and the Magic Pancake Pan

BY

Nick and Tara O'Riley

Illustrated by Matt Loveridge

Copyright © 2014 Nick and Tara O'Riley
All rights reserved.

ISBN: 1493502026
ISBN 13: 9781493502028
Library of Congress Control Number: 2013920043
CreateSpace Independent Publishing Platform
North Charleston, South Carolina

For Finn and Lynnie

ACKNOWLEDGEMENTS

Although Boomish would say that we should be thanking him, we would like to acknowledge the following individuals for helping to make this book a reality:

Lynn B. O'Riley, Antonia & Edward Osgood, Roberta Bishop, Jane Zalman, Steve Kasperowicz, Lindsey Kasperowicz, Patricia Gay Williams, Rowan O'Riley, Trudie O'Riley, Chet Carey, Curtis Ingram, Stephen Gushee, Glenn Berger, Michaela McGivern, Maggie Squires, Amy Stuart, Gregory Cole, and last, but certainly not least, MangyDog – thank you Dog!

We would also like to extend a stupendalous thank you to our supremely talented CreateSpace editor, Lauren P. Your insights, encouragement and expertise were invaluable, and we look forward to working with you again.

A Dark and Sorrowful Night

Desdemona, a sturdy brown mouse wearing an embroidered peasant dress and a red babushka, glanced up from her knitting as a cold draft crept across the smooth, slate floor of the cave. Shivering, she got up from her rocking chair to check on the ancient cat, Betsy, sleeping in the bed nearby.

The cat's breath was weak and wheezy, and her paw felt cold to the touch. Frowning, the mouse pulled the coverlet up over the cat's shoulders. As she did, the large, leather-bound recipe book Betsy had been reading slid down to the cat's stomach. Desdemona glanced down at the open page. "Chocolate fluffles," she said, turning her head toward the cave door. "Fluffles always were Betsy's favorite creation. Weren't they, boys?"

Standing guard on either side of the door were two squat, chocolate-brown dogs with bat ears, Cocoa and Mocha. As usual, they were dressed in the traditional uniform of the

Marzipan Grenadier: red dress coats with gold buttons and fringe, towering bearskin hats, and swords belted around their pudgy bellies.

"Oui, oui," they solemnly agreed.

Desdemona picked up her knitting and was lowering herself into her chair when Betsy slowly and shakily exhaled. The mouse froze, waiting for her old friend to take another wheezy breath. It never came. The next second, the pages of the Master Book of Recipes fluttered as the back cover rose up and over and the book shut itself with a soft *thud* and a tiny *click*.

"She's gone," Desdemona whispered hoarsely. "And with her goes a bit of the sweetness of the islands." The two Grenadiers bowed their heads as the mouse pulled out a hand-kerchief and dabbed her teary eyes. "Betsy was a true friend and the best Master Sweet Smith the Lemon Meringue Islands have ever known. We were lucky to have had her." Cocoa and Mocha nodded, their hats wobbling precariously as their eyes filled with tears.

Tucking her kerchief away, Desdemona gently pulled the covers over Betsy's head. "Good-bye, my dear friend," she whispered.

Cocoa, unable to contain his sorrow, raised his chin to the ceiling and howled, "Owoo!"

Mocha's jowls trembled as he fought to maintain his professionalism, then he too lost control. "Owoo! Owoo!"

Outside, other Marzipan Grenadiers took up the call, and the night air echoed with their howls of sadness. Desdemona waited until their cries had drifted away. Then, tenderly, she lifted the book off the blanket and carried it to a niche on the far side of the room. Propped up inside was a barely vibrating cast iron pancake pan. Placing the book next to the pan, she took a long breath, then turned back to the dogs. "Well, boys," she said, "as much as I hate to say it in this time of sorrow, the baking must go on. It's time to discover the name of the new Master Sweet Smith."

"Oui, Madame," Cocoa said, his ears drooping.

"I know," she said gently. "I'm sad, too. But take heart. I'm sure the next Protector of the Lemon Meringue Islands will be just as wonderful as Betsy was. After all, the magic of the islands has never stirred us wrong. Has it?" The dogs shook their heads. "All right, then," Desdemona said as she took a breath. "Here we go."

She reached out a paw and grabbed the handle of the trembling pancake pan. As soon as she made contact, it began buzzing like a bumblebee. The dogs cocked their heads at the curious sound. With a small grunt, Desdemona slid the pan off the shelf and raised it above her head. Immediately, swirly gold letters began to appear inside, glowing brighter and brighter until finally Desdemona could make out the words. "Boomish K. Sullivan, Dismal Manor, Briarberry," she read.

The next second the pan turned black and the humming noise stopped. Slipping it back into the niche, Desdemona's whiskers twitched thoughtfully. "Boomish K. Sullivan," she said slowly. "Now that sounds like a very special name indeed, don't you think?"

"Oui, oui, Madame," the dogs agreed.

"And Briarberry," she whispered, a faraway look in her eyes. "Why, I haven't been there since I was a lass. If I remember correctly, Dismal Manor is Briarberry's orphanage. This Mister Sullivan must work with the poor orphans," she said, her eyes brightening. "Most likely he's the headmaster, and an especially caring and generous soul. Right, boys?"

The dogs were still nodding when a black-and-white Marzipan Grenadier quickstep marched into the room and saluted. "Yes, Maurice," Desdemona said. "What is it?"

"So many pardons, Madame," he said. "But les Sweet Smiths, they are getting, how you say, confussy?"

"The Smiths are still awake?" Desdemona said. Then she glanced back at the covered form on the bed and shook her head. "Oh. Of course. Betsy didn't—she wasn't able to ring the bedtime bell." Realizing she had another duty to take care of, Desdemona reached for her shawl and wrapped it around her shoulders. "It seems that's all the pity pie we have time for tonight. I'd best give the Smiths the bad news."

She headed out the door and started down a well-trodden dirt path. The Grenadiers hurried after her, each one vying for the coveted heel position at her side. Behind them, the cone-shaped silhouette of the marshmallow-covered Mount Maraschino glowed in the moonlight; its cherry-shaped boulder balancing on its peak.

The trail wound down a grassy hillside covered with chuckleberry, custardberry, and chocolateberry bushes. The orchard came next, its myriad fruit and nut trees hanging so heavy with bounty the dogs had to duck down to keep their hats from being knocked off.

Finally, they reached the back of a long, stone building. Before the other grenadiers had a chance, Cocoa shot forward and grabbed the handle of the thick wooden door. "Le Grand Kitchen!" he announced as he pulled. The door swung open, and Desdemona rubbed her eyes in disbelief.

The normally spotless kitchen was a chaotic mess. Baking tables were covered with splatters, batter-coated spoons, and unfinished desserts. Clouds of flour hung in the air. Broken eggs lay like landmines on the floor. The neatness and order that were Betsy's hallmarks had dissolved into mayhem as dozens of furry, brown, gerbil-like creatures wearing chefs' hats and jackets scampered haphazardly about, dropping pans and bumping into one another. Those who weren't running about stood fixed at their tables, scratching their heads or staring off into space.

As Desdemona and the Grenadiers cautiously stepped inside, a Sweet Smith holding a spatula and a measuring cup zigzagged up to them. "Hi, short lady!" he chirruped, looking behind her expectantly. "Um, where's the Nice Lady? I need to ask her something." He waved his utensils in her face as she struggled to find the right words.

"I'm sorry," Desdemona said finally, "but the Nice Lady won't be coming back anymore." She held her breath waiting for the waterworks, but the creature just smiled and nodded as more Sweet Smiths wandered over.

"Hey! Short lady!" called a Smith covered in flour. "Can you get the Nice Lady? We need to make the birthday cakes!"

Desdemona cleared her throat and said, "Listen, all of you. I can't get the Nice Lady. She...she has gone on to her great reward."

"She got an award?" a Sweet Smith piped, clapping his paws in excitement. The other Smiths *oohed* and *ahhed*.

"No, no." Desdemona shook her head. "What I mean is... she—she is sleeping the endless sleep."

"Well, can you wake her up?" asked a Sweet Smith with batter-caked whiskers. "I need to ask her something."

"Me, too!" chirped another.

"Just wake her up!" demanded a third.

"But I can't wake her up," said Desdemona, throwing her paws in the air.

"Why not?" asked the first Sweet Smith.

"Yeah, why not?" said another.

"Just wake the Nice Lady up!" called another.

"Yeah, wake her up!" demanded a whisk-wielding Smith.

"Wake her up! Wake her up!" the Smiths chanted as Desdemona's calls for quiet grew fainter and fainter in the din.

Finally, she'd had enough. Grabbing two greasy baking sheets from a nearby rack, she banged them together and squeaked, "Quiet everyone!" The Smiths froze, their eyes round. Desdemona lowered the pans and exclaimed, "What I am trying to tell you is that the Nice Lady is dead!"

Her news was met with silence as the creatures looked at one another, some scratching their heads. "Dead?" asked a voice from the back.

"Yes," she exclaimed. "Dead!"

"Awww," they all moaned. Then slowly, their tails dragging through puddles of milk, the Smiths went back to banging and clanging, though not as noisily as before.

"Wait!" Desdemona called after them. "I'm still here, and I know a cup or two about baking. I can help you! At least until we find the next Master Sweet—I mean, Nice Lady!" The Smiths paid no attention and Desdemona's face darkened as she realized how quickly things were falling apart. "Cocoa," she said, "fetch the pan and my traveling bag and meet me at the *Pudding*."

The dog trotted off, and Desdemona led Mocha and Maurice through the long kitchen and out the front entrance that led to the docks. "As the Lemon Meringue Islands' second in command," she said as they hurried down the dark path, "it falls to me to fetch the next Master Sweet Smith. If I don't," she breathed, "desserts in the Bewhiskered Lands will become harder to find than a blueberry in a chuckleberry pie."

When they reached the harbor, Desdemona was surprised to see the torches alight and a group of Grenadiers milling about in front of one of the delivery galleons. Scratching her head, she hurried over.

A black and white Grenadier was on board, raising the flag of the Lemon Meringue Islands, a silver Mount Maraschino topped with a cherry on a royal-blue background. Two others were loading crates marked "Biscuits" onto the ship while a large cream-colored Grenadier holding a clipboard and a feathered quill checked them off his list.

"What in Betsy's name is going on, Cream Puff?" Desdemona asked the dog. "I thought the *Baker's Dozen* was supposed to have sailed yesterday! And where are the birthday cakes?"

"So sorry, Madame," Cream Puff said, his forehead wrinkled with concern. "We wait for ze birthday cakes, but ze Smiths, zey bring us no cakes. So now we sail wizout zem."

Desdemona gasped. "But that means twenty-two critters won't get their birthday cakes!" Cream Puff shrugged apologetically. Realizing there was nothing to be done but fetch the Master Smith as quickly as she could, Desdemona raced down to the end of the dock with Mocha and Maurice in tow and leapt onto an unassuming wooden dory called the *Tasty Pudding.*

She was just raising the sail when a panting Cocoa trotted up. He saluted and passed over a softly humming carpetbag needle-pointed with daisies and roses. After making sure the pan was safely inside, Desdemona stowed the bag in the sleeping compartment below and turned to the dogs. "You all know what a tricky time this is," she said. "With no pan and no Master Smith, the Lemon Meringues will be practically defenseless. So you must be on guard at all times and pray that you-know-who doesn't get a whiff of what's going on."

"Oui, Madame!" the dogs barked.

"Now, I'll be as quick as I can, but since this Mister Sullivan seems to be an animal in a position of importance, it's better to be safe than sorry. Mocha, tell me. Who's our special friend in Briarberry?"

The dog scratched under his hat, then his eyes lit up. "Zat is ze honorable Judge Oddkins, Madame," he replied.

"Judge Oddkins. Of course!" she said. "He'll be sure to have any paperwork we might need and he's an old friend to boot." The dogs wagged their stubby tails in agreement. "Cocoa," she said, locking eyes with him, "you're first in command while I'm away."

"Oui, Madame!"

"Keep things going as best you can, and hopefully I'll be back before the custard sets!" Quickly, Desdemona untied the bow rope, and as the boat sailed out of the harbor, the dogs stood at attention until the *Pudding* was nothing but a dark shadow in the moonlit waters of the Sarsaparilla Sea.

A Dismal Manor

The cavernous dining hall of Dismal Manor rang with the boisterous shouts of skinny, flea-bitten orphans impatiently waiting for their lunch. Two sheep, Sisters Gertrude and Mary Therese, sat at the head table, their lips pursed in perpetual dismay as they nibbled their gruel. Sister Drusilla, a hulking bear with paws the size of baseball mitts, patrolled the rows, the robes of her habit dragging behind her as she went.

Halfway down one of the many overcrowded tables, an orange cat was busily scribbling away on a napkin while nearby orphans giggled. Raising a suspicious eyebrow, Sister Drusilla tromped up behind him as the cat held up the napkin and announced, "And this is my latest masterpiece. It's called, *Sister Dragon Nostrils Taking a Bath.* In a lake. 'Cause she's so big. Get it?"

Thwack!

The cat rubbed his head where Sister Drusilla had smacked him. "Thank you, young Boomish," said the bear, plucking the drawing from his paw. "I'll take that, and I'll see you in the scrub room after dinner."

Shaking her head, she continued down the aisle as Sister Agnes, a lumbering cow, plopped two bowls of gray mush in front of Boomish and the excitable gray hamster, Jack, squirming next to him. "This is absolutely disgustamous," Boomish said, shoving the bowl away. "And I'm not going to take it anymore."

He pushed himself up from the bench, but the hamster threw himself onto the cat's neck. "No, Boom Boom!" Jack squealed. "Every time you complain, they just take away our food! And it's Wesley's birthday, remember?" He frantically pointed across the table at a wire-haired dog with floppy ears whose tail was wagging in anticipation. "If you make any trouble today, Sister Drusilla won't give him his piece of cake!"

Reluctantly, Boomish sat back down. "OK," he grumbled. "But tomorrow, Sister Drusilla is going to get an earful from me." Sighing with relief, Jack let go and slid back onto the bench as Sister Agnes finished serving the mush and clopped out the double doors to the kitchen.

Across the room, Sister Drusilla flicked the head of a ferret who was aiming a spoonful of gruel at the bunny sitting across from him. Rolling her eyes in frustration, she returned to the head table, sat down, bowed her head in prayer, and began to eat.

Hurriedly, the orphans choked down their helpings of slop, then fidgeted restlessly as they waited for Sister Agnes and the birthday cake. Moments later, the Sisters finished their dinner and tried not to drool as they too waited for the cow's return.

After what seemed like an eternity, the double doors swung open and in trotted a concerned-looking Sister Agnes, her hooves empty. Anxious mutterings filled the air as she bent over and whispered in Sister Drusilla's ear. The bear's face fell. All eyes were locked onto Sister Drusilla as she rose from her chair and raised a meaty paw. "Attention everyone," she said. "I have an especially dismal announcement to make."

The orphans exchanged glances.

"What did Boomish do now?" a badger asked his neighbor.

"Shh!" shushed a mouse.

Sisters Gertrude and Mary Therese blinked. Sister Agnes stared at the floor.

"Unfortunately, the delivery from the Lemon Meringue Islands did not arrive," Sister Drusilla said. Cries of disbelief echoed across the room. Jack's mouth dropped open. Boomish frowned as he studied Sister Drusilla's face. "This means," she continued, "Wesley will not get his slice of birthday cake today."

A collective gasp filled the room and all eyes turned towards Wesley, whose lower lip was trembling. Two squirrels, Constance and Francesca, patted him consolingly as Sisters Gertrude and Mary Therese *baaed* in dismay. Some of the younger animals started to cry.

"The Sisters and I will pray for the safe arrival of the birthday cake," Sister Drusilla informed them. "In the meantime, you may all go outside." The orphans, ears drooping and tails hanging, slowly filed out of the dining hall, whispering as they went.

"No delivery?"

"That's what she said."

"But that's impossible!"

As Boomish and Jack got up to go, a raspy voice from behind them said, "Hey Junior, I betcha Poofish here has something to do with the missing birthday cake."

Boomish turned and came face-to-face with Magnus, a flat-faced, slobbery bulldog, and his scrawny sidekick Junior. "You know, Magnus," Boomish said, "I would argue with you, but I don't think your teeny walnut brain would understand what I was saying."

"Besides," Jack chimed in, "Boomish had nothing to do with Wesley's missing cake. You heard Sister Drusilla. The cake wasn't delivered."

"Yeah, well, I don't buy it," Magnus barked. "The Lemon Meringue Islands always deliver on time. Besides, Poofish is always doin' somethin' to get everyone in trouble."

"That's right," Junior yapped. "Like when Boomish put on the play about the mean sister who starved all the orphans and made them work day and night. Sister Drusilla got ma-*ad*, and we got recess taken away for a whole week!"

"That," Boomish shot back, "was a protest to protestate the awful conditions around this dump."

"Bah, you just wanted to show off," Magnus said, foamy flecks of drool spraying from his jowls. "You're always tryin' to be the top cat, and it always ends up getting everyone else detention," he continued. "Well, I've got news for you, cat. There's no such thing as a 'top cat.' There's only a top—uh, a top..."

"Top dog," Junior piped up.

"That's right," Magnus said, and Junior smirked.

Boomish put his paws on his hips. "You know what, Magnus?" he said. "You're nothing but a flea-infested mutt."

"Oh, yeah?" Magnus shot back. "Well, better that than a mangy stray."

"Mutt!"

"Stray!"

"Mutt, mutt!"

"Mangy stray!"

Thwack!

Boomish and Magnus rubbed the sides of their heads where Sister Drusilla's paws made contact. "That's quite enough from both of you," she said, making shooing motions with her paws. "Now get outside before I put you both on pot-scrubbing duty."

Once outside, Boomish and Jack wandered over to a small group of animals gathered around Wesley. "Well, at least we didn't have to sit and watch the Sisters eat the rest of the birthday cake again," Wesley was saying.

"Yeah," said Francesca, "but what about you?"

"You didn't get your piece," chattered Constance.

"I'm hungry!" groaned Morris the pig, cradling his stomach like a baby.

"You're always hungry," Boomish said, as he and Jack walked up. Morris made a pouty face.

"But we're hungry too, Boomish," the squirrels chorused.

"That's because you're squirrels," Boomish said. "You have no reserves."

"Can we talk about something else?" pleaded Wesley. "This conversation really isn't making me feel any better."

Boomish wasn't listening. "You know something?" he said, rubbing his chin thoughtfully with a paw. "An injustimous has happened to our friend that must be justimicated. And I know just how to do it." Jack started hopping and the squirrels clapped their paws, but Wesley and Morris exchanged nervous glances.

"This 'justice getting' that you're talking about. It isn't going to get us in trouble, is it, Boomish?" Wesley asked.

Boomish held a paw to his chest and blinked. "Trouble?" he asked. "Why would my idea get us into trouble?"

"Because that's what your ideas always do!" Morris squealed. Wesley nodded.

"Well, not this time," Boomish insisted. "This is a one-hundred-percent foolproof, no-one-gets-into-any-trouble plan, guaranteed! But," he added, "I guess if you two ladies would feel safer staying here, be my guest." And after glancing about the grounds for any sisters, he casually ambled across the yard with Jack and the squirrels scampering at his heels.

Wesley shook his head as he watched them go. Morris frowned at his rumbling stomach and then looked at Wesley with pleading eyes. The dog avoided his stare for a whole three seconds before he broke down. "Oh, all right," he grumbled. "But don't blame me if Boomish's big idea gets us into trouble—*again*."

They hurried after the others and found them crouched beside the back entrance to the kitchen. "OK, everybody," Boomish whispered, his paw on the doorknob, "follow me." Gingerly, he turned the knob, cracked opened the door, and peeked in. Seeing no one, he slipped inside, motioning for the others to follow. After the last animal was in, he shut the door and hurried across the kitchen to check the hallway that led to the rest of the building. It was empty. Satisfied that the coast was clear, Boomish turned around and surveyed his domain.

"Smells like Sister Agnes has already put the soup on," he said, waving a paw in front of his nose at the fishy aroma filling the room. "So we should have a good hour or two before she comes back."

Chest out, Boomish strode across the room, lifted an apron and a chef's hat off the counter, and ceremoniously put them on. At once, he was transformed. His eyes narrowed and with laser-like focus, he zipped about the kitchen pulling out pots, pans, and utensils while the other animals looked on in amazement.

Once Boomish had assembled his tools, Wesley spoke up. "Um, Boomish," he said, "would you mind telling us what we're doing in the kitchen?"

The cat's mouth dropped open. "Wasn't anybody listening?" he cried, looking at the group. A sea of blank faces stared back. "We're baking Wesley a birthday cake! The biggest, most humungomous birthday cake the Bewhiskered Lands have ever seen!"

"Goody!" cried Jack, and the squirrels clapped their paws.

"But, Boomish," Morris said, scratching his head, "nobody can make a birthday cake. Well, nobody but the giant, two-headed flying iguana who lives on the Lemon Meringue Islands."

The squirrels giggled behind their paws and Wesley snorted, "Flying iguana! Have you been listening to Magnus again? Everyone knows the desserts are made by the old, warty Gingerbread Witch and her singing toadfish!"

"What's a toadfish?" asked Jack.

"It's half fish, half—"

"Silence!" Boomish demanded. "You're ruining my moment." The animals mumbled their apologies. Pacified, Boomish picked up a mixing spoon and pointed it at Morris. "You, pig," he ordered, "get me all the cans of Frominoff's Sliced Savory you can find. Wesley, I need cheese. You three," he pointed to Jack and the squirrels, "I need olives, mayonnaise, and tomatoes." He tapped his chin. "And a carrot!"

The animals scrambled to collect their ingredients, then piled them on the baking table. Boomish studied them critically. "I can work with this," he said with a nod. Then shooing his assistants back with his paws he said, "Stand back, everybody, and get ready to see genius in action!"

The animals did as they were told, and Boomish went to work. His paws flew as he darted back and forth filling pans, stacking layers, swirling mayonnaise, slicing cheese, and carving garnishes.

Jack hopped as high as he could, trying to catch a glimpse of the action. The squirrels leapt onto the pot rack for a better view. Morris stared with his mouth open while drool dribbled down Wesley's chin.

When Boomish was done, he stood back to admire his work. Taller than Francesca, the cake was five tiers high. Its shiny swirls of mayonnaise frosting were adorned with roses carved out of tomatoes. Around the sides, miniature carrot stick figures of Boomish, Wesley and Jack, struck poses on a ship made out of tiny cheese squares. On top of the cake, olives spelled out the words "Hapi Burthday Weslee". "Oooo," everyone murmured.

"Behold!" Boomish crowed. "The most beautiful cake in the world!" Wiping his mayonnaise-coated paws on his apron he added, "I was born to do this." The others nodded their heads.

"OK, let's eat," Morris grunted. He picked up a serving knife and handed it to Boomish.

Wesley ran to fetch the plates, his tail wagging broadly while the squirrels dropped down from the pot rack. "Let's sing Happy Birthday!" Jack exclaimed.

Boomish pulled off his chef's hat and considered his latest creation. "You know..." he said slowly. Wesley's tail stopped wagging. A look of alarm crossed Morris's face. "...I like the idea of singing Happy Birthday, it's just that..."

"Oh boy, here it comes," said Morris.

Boomish silenced him with a look and continued, "It's just too bad that we're the only ones who get to see the cake."

Jack tugged on his friend's shirt. "But, Boom Boom, you said the cake was for Wesley—for his birthday."

"And it is!" Boomish said, taken aback. "And that's why the other orphans should be here—to help him celebrate.'"

"Tsk, tsk, tsk," Constance scolded. "You never said a word about that before."

"That's right!" said Francesca.

"You just want everyone to see it so you can show off," Morris said.

"Well, that's just not true," Boomish insisted. "What I did, I did because it was a super nice thing to do. And all I want now is to share that super nice thing with everyone else so they can experience the, uh, super niceness as well." He looked around at their incredulous faces. "Jeesh!" he said. "Can you blame a guy for just wanting to share?"

"I can when your sharing is going to get us all in trouble," Wesley said. "You can't parade the whole orphanage through here and expect Sister Drusilla not to notice."

"What do you think I've got floating around up here?" Boomish demanded, tapping between his ears. "Dust bunnies?" He shook his head. "They're called brains. And I've got more of them than all the animals in Dismal Manor put together." Wesley rolled his eyes. Boomish ignored him and continued. "It's simple. We send out the squirrels—they're the fastest, and they're also below the sisters' line of sight."

Constance and Francesca clasped each other's paws and hopped up and down in a seesaw motion. "They bring in the orphans in ones and twos, except for Magnus and Junior of course," Boomish added, making a prune face. Jack, Wesley, and Morris made their own prune faces as well. Boomish leaned closer. "Then, when everyone's here, we'll sing 'Happy Birthday' and pass out the cake." Morris rubbed his tummy and licked his lips. Jack's eyes lit up, and Wesley's tail began to wag again.

"Why, it'll be a party. A super, stupendalous party!" Boomish exclaimed. "And everyone will love me!" he added, hugging himself until the raised eyebrows of Wesley, Morris, and Jack caught his attention. Dropping his arms, he continued, "I mean the party, of course. Everyone will love *the party*."

"Well," Wesley said, "it sure would be nice if everyone could be here and have some cake."

"Of course it would," Boomish said. "Then it's settled. Constance, Francesca, go get the other animals. But remember, no more than two at a time."

"Goody!" squealed the squirrels, hopping over one another in their haste to get out the door.

Within a minute Constance was back, bounding into the kitchen with two confused-looking rabbits. Instantly she spun around and leapt out the door in a frenzy to bring in more animals. Boomish jumped onto the baking table. "Behold!" he cried, presenting the cake with a flourish of his paws. "The

Bestest, Most Bounteous and Beautiful Birthday Cake Ever, made by yours truly, Boomish K. Sullivan!"

"Ahem!" came a voice from below.

Boomish looked down at a frowning Jack. "What?" he said. The hamster pointed at Wesley. "Oh," Boomish said. "Right." He started again. "Behold! The Bestest, Most Bounteous and Beautiful Birthday Cake Ever, made by Boomish K. Sullivan, for Wesley!" The rabbits gasped and thumped their hind feet with all their might. Boomish beamed.

Each time a new orphan was led into the kitchen, Boomish repeated his announcement; sometimes remembering the cake was for Wesley and sometimes not. Soon the room was jam packed with animals gawking at the cake and chattering in amazement.

Outside, Francesca darted about the nearly deserted play yard. She turned a corner and saw Junior and Magnus looking around and scratching their heads. Crinkling her nose, she turned to head back to the kitchen and hopped straight into the bottom half of one last animal. "Oh!" she chirped, grabbing its paw and pulling it along. "Come on, come on! You don't want to miss the party." As she opened the kitchen door, the animals started singing "Happy Birthday" interspersed with barks, howls, moos, and clucks.

"Oh, they've started," squeaked the squirrel. "Hurry now! Let's get to the front!" Pulling the animal along behind her by its paw, she pushed her way through the chanting crowd. Boomish was still on the table, waving a carrot like a conductor's baton, occasionally pointing at Wesley, but mostly crooning to his exquisite creation.

Frantic that she'd miss the big finale, the squirrel pushed and pushed, the animal's paw clutched firmly in her grasp. "Wait! Wait for us!" she cried.

Orphans looked up and froze as they passed. A small bunny fell backward in a dead faint. A strange hush fell over the room, and by the time she and the paw reached the baking table, Boomish was the only one still singing. Francesca dropped the paw and clapped wildly while Boomish held his arms out to his cake singing, "*Happy Birth*...day, tooo..." He swung his arms toward the crowd, "YOUU—*aack*!" he croaked as his paws smacked into the flaring nostrils of Sister Drusilla. "Crivvens!" he squeaked. "Sister Drusilla! What an unexpected—yikes!"

Without a word, the bear grabbed Boomish by the scruff of the neck, hoisted him off the table, and marched him out of the kitchen, her robes sweeping past a sea of terrified faces as she went. The party was over.

A Sweet for the Sour

Captain Blackpaw, a beautiful white cat with sparkling blue eyes, sighed as she sat at her desk, her chin resting on a white paw. Always conscious of her appearance, she wore the finest pirate garb money could buy: black breeches and shiny black boots, a white silk blouse—the ruffles of which puffed out from under a black velvet waistcoat trimmed in gold—and to top off the look, a black tricorn hat embellished with a blue satin sash that brought out the color of her eyes.

Restlessly, her one black paw toyed with a pile of gold coins and jewels strewn atop the desk. Pursing her lips, she flicked a ruby, sending it flying through the air into one of many overflowing treasure chests shoved against the walls. She picked up a gold coin and was about to thwack it when her stomach rumbled. Frowning, she looked down. "Hungry, are we?" she asked, giving her flat stomach a tender pat. "Well how would Captain's tum tum like a little treat?" Shooting a quick glance at the cabin door, Blackpaw hurried over to a large painting of a matronly-looking cat wearing a bonnet. "I'm having a little treat, Mother," she said with a sneer. "You don't mind, do you?"

She lifted the picture off the wall and dropped it to the floor, staring greedily at the safe that had been hidden behind it. Licking her lips, she spun the dial this way and that until she heard a *click*, then pulled open the door. Inside was a single caramel ChewMe. Blackpaw snatched the candy out of the safe and stared at it, dumbfounded that a safe once packed full of candy could be empty so soon. Seething, her blue eyes saw red, and she was about to scream with rage when—*Knock! Knock! Knock!* Quickly, Blackpaw stuffed the candy into a pocket, shut the safe's door, and re-hung the painting. Hurrying back to her chair, she smoothed her whiskers. "Enter," she said.

Slowly, the door swung open, and in sidled her first mate, Jeremiah the muskrat. Dressed in a dirty nightshirt and baggy breeches, he slid a woolen cap off his head and fidgeted excitedly. "Well?" Blackpaw demanded.

"Yes, Captain," Jeremiah said brightly, dancing from foot to foot. "I just wanted to report that I spied a small skiff off the starboard bow, yes I did!"

"And?"

"And?" Jeremiah scratched his head. "Oh! Well, would you like me to tell the boys to prepare a raiding party?" He nodded hopefully. Blackpaw's azure eyes narrowed, and Jeremiah's smile faded.

"A raiding party? For a small skiff?" She exposed her claws and began tapping the desk, a cold look in her eyes.

Jeremiah began to wish he'd never knocked on her door. "Well, I just thought, since we're pirates and, well, being pirates we should—"

Blackpaw cut him off. "Jeremiah," she said icily, "I thought I made myself perfectly clear: No. Small. Potatoes."

"Aye, aye, Captain," Jeremiah nodded as if his life depended on it. "You was most certainly clear on that point. It's just... I mean, I don't want to be uppity or forget my place or..."

"Out with it, Jeremiah."

"It's just, well, you've gone and raided every *big* ship and stronghold in these Bewhiskered Lands and..."—Blackpaw raised an eyebrow—"and," he continued hesitantly, "well, Captain, um, there just ain't no *big* potatoes left." As Blackpaw stood up, Jeremiah threw his paws above his head to block the blow he knew was coming. But the cat picked her way around piles of gold bars and precious stones to the map of the Bewhiskered Lands hanging on the cabin wall.

Red Xs marking Blackpaw's conquests peppered the map like the spots on a Dalmatian. Xs were stamped on every ship in every ocean, sea, and river. Every seaside town had an X. Some had two. Only one spot was X free: the Lemon Meringue Islands. Blackpaw examined the map thoughtfully. "Perhaps I've done too good of a job," she muttered.

"Aw, no, Captain. I wouldn't say that," Jeremiah said, chuckling good-naturedly.

Blackpaw turned, her paws on her hips. "Really? You think I *haven't* done a good job?"

"What?" he gasped. "Oh! No, no! So sorry, Captain!" The muskrat whacked himself on the head and added, "You get ol' Jerry talking, and pretty soon he gets himself all confused, and the next thing you know—"

"Relax, Jeremiah," Blackpaw interrupted, turning back to the map. "No one's walking the plank...yet." Exhaling with relief, Jeremiah shuffled over to her side. Blackpaw rested a paw on his head and drummed her nails, deep in thought. "Maybe I *have* done too good of a job," she said finally.

Jeremiah carefully kept his mouth shut while his eyes jumped from one red X to another. Then he spied the Lemon Meringue Islands, and his face lit up. "Captain, I've got a clever idea, yes I do."

Blackpaw stopped drumming. "Umm?"

Jeremiah pointed excitedly at the map. "Why don't we raid the Lemon Meringue—"

Whack! Blackpaw's blow sent Jeremiah flying across the room. He landed headfirst in a pile of gold coins. "Oh, Jeremiah," she crooned. "Dear, sweet, forgetful Jeremiah. We've been over this before, haven't we?"

Jeremiah sat up and rubbed his head. "Aye, Captain. It's coming back to ol' Jerry now."

"No one is to mention that infernal place in my presence." Blackpaw said, her eyes flashing. "Not until I've found a way to breach its defenses, that is. But I simply refuse to attack again until they fight fair."

"Too right, Captain. Too right," Jeremiah agreed. "All that magic. Bah! It's cheatin' is what it is. Why, it's just not fair."

"Not fair," Blackpaw muttered to herself. "I know a thing or two about not fair. Why, my whole life's been unfair!" And as the first mate babbled on, memories of all those unfair times came flooding back to Blackpaw.

How Unfairness Drove Sweet Kitten Nancy to Become the Villainous Captain Blackpaw

Exhibit A: The Chocolate Cake Incident

A dirt-coated Kitten Blackpaw squirmed in her seat, her mouth watering as she waited for dessert. Sitting next to her, his paws folded politely in his lap, was her little brother Francis. Francis looked over at his sister and smiled sweetly. Kitten Blackpaw stuck out her tongue.

A second later, Mother Cat swept into the room holding a dome-covered cake stand and set it on the table. "Here we are," she sang. "Fresh from the Lemon Meringue Islands." She lifted the dome to reveal a beautiful, three-layer chocolate cake.

"Yippee!" cried Francis. "Thank you most awfully, Mother."

Kitten Blackpaw greedily licked her lips as her mother placed a towering slice of cake on her brother's plate. He purred gratefully, and Mother Cat patted his head.

Impatiently, Blackpaw shoved her plate forward, but Mother Cat picked up the dome and dropped it over the cake. "I'm sorry to disappoint you, Nancy," she said. "But after the day you've given me, there will be no cake for you."

Kitten Blackpaw scowled as Francis daintily ate his cake and hummed, "Mmmm!"

Exhibit B: The Doughnuts and Cocoa Incident

Young Blackpaw watched from the doorway as Francis sat at the kitchen table smiling sweetly, a plate of doughnuts in front of him. Mother Cat poured him a cup of cocoa, patted his head, and went back to the stove. As soon as her mother's back was turned, Blackpaw, her nose scratched and the sleeve of her dress torn, slunk into the kitchen and slipped into her chair.

When her mother returned with more doughnuts, Blackpaw thrust out her plate. Mother Cat took one look at her and threw up her paws. "Fighting again, Nancy?" she cried. "And on Sunday. For shame! Well, if you think you're going to get doughnuts and cocoa after skipping church and engaging in fisticuffs, you are sorely mistaken."

Blackpaw sat fuming as Francis nibbled his doughnuts and cried, "Yummy!"

Exhibit C: A Case of Candy Kleptomania

Teenage Blackpaw paced back and forth in front of a candy shop, glancing into the window now and again. When the last customer exited, she casually strolled inside. Moments later she bolted out of the store, her arms full of candy and an angry shopkeeper on her heels.

"Stop! Thief!" he yelled, brandishing a broom.

Exhibit D: D is For the Dumb Dumb Who Sent Me to Jail

Teenage Blackpaw, her fur matted beneath the yellow flower-print prison uniform she wore, stood in a courtroom before Judge Oddkins, a kindly looking badger in a black robe and spectacles. He sighed heavily as he studied her rap sheet.

"Well, well, well," he said to himself. "Oh my. My, my, my. Dear, dear, dear." Lowering his spectacles, he addressed the cat. "Well, well, well," he said. "So much trouble for such a young lady." Blackpaw gave him the evil eye. Judge Oddkins sighed. "As much as I hate to do it," he said, "I must act in your best interest. Therefore, I sentence you to Miss Felicity's Facility for Felonious Female Felines." Teenage Blackpaw glared at him defiantly. "Is there anything you would like to say before you are taken away?" the judge asked gently.

"Just this," Blackpaw spat. "You've not seen the last of me. If you think you can keep me from my precious desserts, you're wrong. Mark my words. One day you'll all be *very, very sorry*." Judge Oddkins gave the signal and two pig bailiffs stepped forward. Blackpaw saw them coming and yelled, "You'll all get your just desserts! You'll see! One day it will be *me* controlling the Lemon Meringue Islands. *Me!*"

The pigs each grabbed an arm and dragged Blackpaw, hissing and spitting, down the aisle. "I will have my cake and eat it tooo!" she screeched as the courtroom doors slammed shut behind her.

Exhibit E: Why Using Magic to Fight Your Battles is
CHEATING!

Captain Blackpaw stood at the helm of the black brigantine *Cat O' Nine Tails*, her motley crew of pirates at their battle stations and Jeremiah at her side. Her eyes gleamed as she spun the wheel and sailed full speed toward the Lemon

Meringue Islands. "I shall have my cake and eat it too!" she cried.

As the *Cat* sped toward the harbor, Blackpaw saw nothing but peacefully moored boats and cloud-covered hillsides. Grinning, she cried, "Ha! Those cream puffs don't even know we're coming. This is going to be a cakewalk." Suddenly, Blackpaw caught sight of a serenely smiling cat standing on a bluff raising a cast iron pan. As the pan rose up, the clouds lifted from the hills to reveal ranks of Marzipan Grenadiers standing next to rows of giant catapults.

The pan-wielding cat gave the signal, and the Grenadiers fired at will. Blackpaw shrieked with rage and spun the wheel, trying to dodge the onslaught of sticky marshmallow goo blobs sailing through the air. But she was too late. With one swipe of her paw, the Master Smith defeated Blackpaw and sent her limping home to lick her sticky wounds.

Blackpaw relaxed her clenched jaw as Jeremiah's voice brought her back to the present. "After all, fair is fair, and—"

"Jeremiah," she said, "tell Mister Growley to set a course for Heckler's Hunch. If there are any big potatoes left to dig up, that's where I'll hear about them. Besides," she added, her stomach rumbling at the thought of the empty safe, "I'm running low on supplies."

Jeremiah clapped his paws excitedly. "Oh, Captain," he cried. "Are we to have a bit of shore leave?"

"Call it what you like," she answered. "Just don't draw attention to yourselves while we're there."

"A heart of gold you have, Captain. Yes, sir, solid gold!" He did a little dance and turned to go.

"And make sure to disguise the crew and the ship," Blackpaw called as he danced out of the cabin.

"Aye, aye, Captain! Aye..."

Thud! The second the door closed, Blackpaw unwrapped the caramel ChewMe and stuffed it into her mouth, glaring at the Lemon Meringue Islands on the map as she chewed. "Il nt waste m'time n yu agin. Nt whle th oddsr nfrly stckd agns me." She slurped and then swallowed. "But I'm a patient cat," she said. "I can wait."

Master Smith Theater

Desdemona nodded in satisfaction as she steered the *Tasty Pudding* between the stone breakwaters of Briarberry's busy harbor. "Right on schedule," she said to herself in relief.

As she got up to lower the sail, a passing fishing boat glided by on its way out to sea. Desdemona hugged the mast as its wake bounced the *Pudding* like a fishing bob. Once the boat stopped rocking, the mouse pulled out the oars and rowed down the crowded docks, looking for an empty spot. Finally, she found one and squeezed the *Pudding* in.

After securing the boat, Desdemona headed below to fetch the carpetbag. Pulling it out, she noticed the humming sound was louder than before. "Yes, we're getting closer, aren't we?" she said to the pan. Sticking an arm through the handles of the bag, she slid it over her shoulder and leapt onto the pier.

As she hurried toward town, Desdemona glanced across the water at the cobblestone streets and wooden storefronts of

Briarberry. Animals dressed in their town finery carried shopping baskets and hurried from store to store. Others window-shopped or chatted on the wooden sidewalks. At the far end of town, the old factories were still puffing smoke from their stone chimneys.

"It's hard to believe it's been so long since I've been here," Desdemona said. "Everything looks exactly the—oh." A group of grumbling animals stood in front of Mama Moo Moo's Bakery shaking their paws at a sign in the window. "No Birthday Cakes So Stop Asking!" it read. Desdemona frowned. "Goodness," she murmured, "I'd best hustle buns. I've no time to waste."

She quickened her pace, weaving her way down the crowded streets until she came to a crossroads. Taking a breath, she glanced at the street signs then turned down Prickly Place, studying the buildings carefully as she went. "That one looks familiar," she said, eyeing a narrow, two-story building on the right. Brick steps led up to the stoop, and a sign above the door read, "Oddkins, Bodkins, and Hootenstein, Attorneys at Law."

"That's it," Desdemona said as she hopped up the steps and rang the small brass bell hanging next to the door. A moment later footsteps sounded inside, and an elderly badger wearing spectacles swung open the door.

"My, my, Desdemona!" exclaimed Judge Oddkins, blinking in astonishment. "Well, well, well. Come in, come in." He smiled broadly as he waved Desdemona inside. "To what do I owe the honor of your visit?"

As Desdemona stepped past him into the foyer, the buzzing of the pan caught his ear, and his smile faded. "Unfortunately, this is not a social call," she said, confirming the badger's suspicions.

"So I hear," the judge said, eyeing the bag. "My, my, my." He removed his glasses and wiped his small eyes. "So Betsy's gone?" he asked. Desdemona nodded and swallowed the lump in her throat.

"Well, well," Judge Oddkins said after a moment. "I suppose I'll get my briefcase."

Due to Desdemona's urgent prodding, Judge Oddkins waddled much faster than usual, and the pair reached the looming gates of Dismal Manor quicker than a Smith could bake a pie. Desdemona's whiskers twitched nervously as they waited for someone to answer the bell.

"Now, now, I hope I have all the necessary documents," said the judge as he rifled through his papers. "After all, I've been semiretired for quite a few years now."

"Yes, yes," Desdemona answered, ringing the bell again. "But the Bewhiskered Lands are running out of desserts as we speak. We must get this Mister Sullivan to the Lemon Meringues as soon as possible. Oh, thank Betsy! Here comes someone."

Judge Oddkins glanced up from his briefcase to see a shabbily dressed rat sauntering up to the gate. "Visiting hours are over," sneered the rat. "Everyone's eatin' dinner. Come back tomorrow."

He turned to go, but Desdemona said quickly, "I'm afraid this can't wait. We must speak with Boomish K. Sullivan. Your headmaster?"

The rat froze. Slowly he turned back around and looked the two visitors up and down. "What are you, pullin' my tail or somethin'?" he asked.

Judge Oddkins cleared his throat and pushed up his spectacles. "I assure you, young man, this is no joke. Take us to your headmaster immediately."

The rat stifled a guffaw, then keeping his head down, he lifted the latch and let them in. "Follow me," he croaked, barely containing his laughter. Doubled-over and shaking, he led them toward the building.

Sisters Drusilla, Agnes, Gertrude, and Mary Therese smiled blissfully as they chewed their food in the unusually quiet dining hall. Leaning forward, Sister Drusilla cupped a hairy paw behind her ear and reveled in the downcast silence filling the room. Sighing contentedly, she picked up her fork and went back to her meal.

Boomish and Jack slouched in their seats, their untouched soup growing cold. The other animals sat as far from them as possible, which, due to the overcrowded nature of the orphanage, wasn't very far. Every so often, somebody shot Boomish a dirty look or whispered an insult. Boomish simply shook his head. He couldn't understand why everyone was so ungrateful when all he'd tried to do was spread a little sunshine around.

At the table behind them, Magnus loudly slurped the last puddles of gravy off his plate, then poked Junior in the ribs.

"Hey, Junior," he said over his shoulder so Boomish would hear. "I think Poofish needs a new nickname. Hmm...." He scratched his head. "How about, Mangy Stray Who Always Gets Everyone In Trouble Except For Me and Junior. Har har har!" he snorted, gravy shooting out his nose.

"Hee hee hee," Junior giggled. "Good one, Magnus."

Jack whipped around and pointed a tiny gray paw in Magnus's face. "You leave Boomish alone!"

"You know what, Jack?" Wesley interrupted. "As much as I hate to admit it, old Slobber Face is right." His fur bristled as he glared at Boomish and said, "Because Mister Big Shot here just *had* to show the whole orphanage his cake, we got caught. And now everyone but those two," he shot a scornful glance across the row, "has to scrub the whole orphanage from top to bottom and eat nothing but soup for a whole month."

Morris covered his face with his hooves. "Soup for a month," he wailed. "How will I survive? I'll wither away to nothing!"

"Not likely," Boomish mumbled.

"Aren't you even sorry you got us all in trouble?" demanded a beaver.

"Yeah. You're not even sorry," called someone else from a table across the room.

"Not sorry! Not sorry!" scolded Constance and Francesca, stamping their paws on the bench.

Over at the head table, Sister Drusilla scowled, unhappy that her precious peace and quiet was already being disturbed.

"Well, if we're going to start pointing paws—" Boomish began, but before he could finish, the double doors burst open, and in stumbled the hunched-over rat followed by Desdemona and Judge Oddkins.

"What now?" exclaimed the bear.

"Sister Drusilla," wheezed the rat, his face contorted by his efforts to keep from laughing, "these two want to see the headmaster." He covered his mouth with a scrawny paw and shook as the entire room stared at the newcomers.

Sister Drusilla eyed the rat suspiciously as she strode toward Desdemona and Judge Oddkins. Quickly, the judge pulled some papers out of his briefcase and held them out to her.

"I'm sorry," the bear said, frowning down her muzzle at the paperwork. "I must've misheard. Who did you say you were looking for?"

"Your headmaster?" Desdemona said a bit uncertainly. "Boomish K. Sullivan." The room exploded in laughter. The rat fell to the floor, tears streaming from his eyes as he gasped for air. Boomish crossed his arms and did a slow burn, insulted that everyone found the idea so funny.

Jack gasped in awe. "You're the headmaster, Boom Boom?"

Realizing her mistake, Desdemona cleared her throat. "I see Mister Sullivan is not your headmaster," she said, looking around at the animals snorting and guffawing with glee. "But as we're in a bit of a hurry, perhaps you could tell me where I might find him."

"Yes, yes," said Judge Oddkins, nodding. "Time is of the essence, don't you know."

Sister Drusilla clasped her paws together in an attempt to control her rising temper. "*Mister* Sullivan, as you call him, is one of my charges," she said. "Therefore you must follow the proper procedure and report to my office during visiting hours with the required paperwork."

"One of your charges?" repeated Desdemona. "You mean he's an orphan?" Sister Drusilla shook her head in disbelief as Desdemona scanned the sea of dirty faces for the next Master Sweet Smith.

"Did you hear that, Judge Oddkins?" Desdemona prompted. "It seems I'll be taking an orphan home with me." The animals gasped. Boomish's eyes grew round, and Jack let out a nervous hiccup.

"Oh!" Judge Oddkins said, taking the hint. "An orphan, did you say? My, my, isn't this a surprise!" He stuffed the headmaster paperwork back into his briefcase and pawed around for the forms pertaining to orphans.

Desdemona meanwhile, sprung into action. Keeping one ear tuned to the humming in the bag, she started down the first table, hunting for Boomish. As she hurried past the orphans, the pan continued to buzz evenly, and she reached the end with no success. Incensed by Desdemona's disregard for the rules, Sister Drusilla started after her, a crazed look on her face. "This is all highly irregular!" she bellowed, her nostrils flaring. "You must stop this immediately!"

Over at the head table, Sisters Agnes, Gertrude, and Mary Therese exchanged looks of alarm and hurried to intercept the tramping bear. Judge Oddkins finally located the correct papers and trotted after the others, waving the forms above his head.

As Desdemona made the turn around the end of the second table, the towering shape of the storming bear caught her eye. "Goodness!" she cried, her eyes wide. Quickening her pace, she scampered down the aisle between Boomish's and Magnus's tables, and the buzzing of the pan grew louder. Nearby orphans cocked their heads at the sound. "Thank Betsy, I'm almost there," Desdemona panted as she passed one eager face after another. Suddenly, the pan's ringing rose to the pitch of an excited mosquito. The mouse skidded to a stop and held her breath as she studied the two animals on either side of her, one of whom was to be the next Master Sweet Smith. To her left, an orange cat stared at her expectantly. On her right was a slobbery, heavily panting dog.

Behind her, Sister Drusilla was closing the gap as Sisters Gertrude, Agnes, and Mary Therese clung to the back of her robe, fighting to slow the bear down. "Please, Sister," mooed Sister Agnes, "remember your vows!"

Almost out of time, Desdemona slid the bag from her shoulder and, keeping the pan inside, held it over Magnus's block-like head. The pan stopped humming. Exhaling with relief, she swung the pan over Boomish's head and, *zaa-riing!* The pan sang, piercing the air with a sound like the whistling of a teakettle. Leaving no room for doubt, Desdemona peeked inside. The pan was glowing gold. "Well," Desdemona said to Boomish. "It looks like it's you."

"Of course it's me," Boomish said. "Who else would it be?"

"Aw, I don't believe it," Magnus spat.

"Well, believe it," said the cat, jumping up and giving him a raspberry. "It's *me*!"

Jack jumped up and down on the bench, his face stretched in a huge smile. The orphans clapped and cheered, partly because they were happy Boomish wouldn't be getting them into any more trouble, but mostly because they couldn't stand Magnus.

Judge Oddkins finally caught up to Sister Drusilla and held out the forms. The bear was about to smack them away, when a look of realization crossed her face. Boomish was about to be taken off her paws.

Boomish leapt onto the dining table and began to dance. Animals shielded their faces as his happy feet sent soup bowls flying.

"My, my," Judge Oddkins exclaimed, clapping in time to Boomish's kicking feet. "I didn't know there would be entertainment."

Desdemona froze, dumbfounded, as Boomish burst into song. "I knew that I was special, much better than the rest," he crooned. "And now that I am leaving, here's something I'll confess. Hey, Magnus, you're breath is stinky! Hey, Sister, your food's the worst! If I had to eat much more of it, I'd leave here in a hearse. It's me! It's me! Don't you see that it just had to be? So now I'll say, 'Good-bye,' and Magnus don't you cry. Adios and c'est la vie. It's me!" His song finished, Boomish did jazz hands and grinned from ear to ear.

Desdemona and Judge Oddkins exchanged stupefied glances while a serene Sister Drusilla plucked the paperwork from the badger's paw. "Where do I sign?" she said with a grin.

Blackpaw Has a Hunch

O f all the towns in the Bewhiskered Lands, Heckler's Hunch was the last place a respectable animal would want to wind up. Its slapdash buildings clung to the rocky coast like hermit crabs. The streets were dark and narrow, and animals there never travelled alone after dark. A popular haunt for sea scum and land rats alike, Heckler's Hunch was a place where decent folk kept their ears down and their noses to themselves. It was, however, the perfect place for Blackpaw's purposes, and as she steered the *Cat O' Nine Tails* through the muddy waters of the harbor, she licked her lips in anticipation of the special supplies she was planning on procuring.

Her crew skulked about the deck, securing sails and un-coiling the bow and stern ropes. Following orders, they had disguised themselves as farmers, replacing their pirate garb with straw hats, plaid shirts, and overalls. "Switch the flag," ordered Blackpaw as she eased the *Cat* around a rickety, old fishing trawler.

A one-eyed weasel, a piece of wheat clamped between his teeth, lowered the Jolly Roger from the main mast and wrinkled his nose as he raised its replacement: a pink flag bedazzled with a diamond tiara.

As the ship pulled up to the dock, an old sea dog mending a fishing net eyed the gold lettering on the ship's hull suspiciously. "Lower the banner," Blackpaw called. A fuchsia and gold banner with the words "Pink Princess" dropped down to hide the name *Cat O' Nine Tails*.

The old sea dog's mouth formed an O, then chuckling with relief, he went back to his mending.

"Ah, Heckler's Hunch," Jeremiah sighed, waddling up to Blackpaw as she pulled on a pair of work gloves. "It's just like coming home."

"I suppose," Blackpaw answered, shoving a straw hat at him, "if your home is riddled with fleas and full to bursting with competitors trying to steal your business." Her cowboy boots clomped loudly as Jeremiah put on his disguise and followed her to the gangplank. "Now remember, Jeremiah," she said. "Keep your ears pricked for any useful information, and report back to me immediately."

"Aye, aye, Captain. Aye, aye," Jeremiah said.

"And don't fill up on fizzle beer and chocolate fluffles," Blackpaw said. "I'm not nursing any upset tummies this time."

"Right, Captain. Ooh, I can hardly wait! We've been too long at sea." He did a happy dance. "Oo! I wonder if they'll have any custardberry pie or maybe a bit of the ol' sugarsnap spice cake."

"Remember, Jeremiah," Blackpaw said, "*you're* here for information, not confections."

They crossed the gangplank and clomped down the dock, stepping over the occasional hole where the wood had rotted through. Ahead of them, a crowd of tail-wagging townsfolk was eagerly watching the unloading of a Lemon Meringues dessert-delivery galleon. Jeremiah licked his lips. Blackpaw's eyes grew round before she quickly turned away. "Oo! Oo! A delivery!" Jeremiah clapped his paws. "Captain, couldn't we get the crew a little treat? Just this once?"

Blackpaw stopped and gave the muskrat a warning look. "Need I remind you of the rules, Jeremiah?"

"Oh no, Captain," Jeremiah said, ducking his head and wincing in anticipation of the memory-jogging blow he was sure was coming. "I remember, yes, I do. No sweets on board."

"Correct," Blackpaw said. "Unless they're for the captain," she added under her breath. She turned and continued clomping, casting a disdainful eye at the crowd as they passed. Many of the onlookers drooled uncontrollably as a pair of Grenadiers dropped a crate marked "Biscuits" onto the dock. "I, Jeremiah," Blackpaw told him, "have what's called self-control. That's something everyone but me seems to lack. If I allowed treats on board the *Cat,* you'd all stuff yourselves silly. It would be disgusting. Nobody would get any work done. Now, where was I? Oh, yes. Now, Jeremiah..."

But Jeremiah had disappeared. Blackpaw glanced around and finally spotted him in the middle of the dessert crowd. Furious, she stormed over as the Grenadiers dropped another crate of biscuits next to the first.

"OK. Allez, allez! Time to go," said Cream Puff as he checked off his clipboard.

Disgruntled mutterings spread through the crowd. "Wait a minute," barked an Irish wolfhound wearing an apron. "Where's the rest of it?"

"Yes, where are all the desserts?" demanded a plump Persian cat waving a mixing spoon threateningly.

The two Marzipan Grenadiers who had unloaded the crates exchanged nervous glances and hurriedly prepared for departure. "I am tres sorry," Cream Puff said, tucking away his clipboard and quickly untying the rope from the dock. "But I don't speak English, so unfortunately I cannot understand what you're saying."

"Well, then what's that you're speaking right now?" demanded the wolfhound.

Cream Puff froze on the gangplank he was crossing. "I mean to say, we have une petite snafu," he said. The other two Grenadiers smiled and nodded as they raised the sails. "That is all," called Cream Puff as he pulled up the gangplank. "Nothing to worry for. Everything will be back to normal next time for sure. But for now we say, 'Au revoir and bon voyage!'" He dabbed his forehead with a hankie as their ship pulled away from the pier.

"Are reeveeare, my eye," said the wolfhound, shaking a fist at them. "I've got four banquets this week! What am I supposed to do about the dessert? Throw out a handful of biscuits and yell, 'Come and get it!'?"

The cat waddled after them until she ran out of dock. "What do you expect me to do with biscuits?" she yelled. "My customers don't want biscuits!" She hurled her spoon after the ship. The Marzipan Grenadiers ducked, then smiled and waved.

Blackpaw, who'd been watching the proceedings with interest, had seen enough. She took hold of Jeremiah's ear and pulled him away from the agitated crowd. "Oo! Ouch, Captain! That's ol' Jerry's ear you've got there," Jeremiah said, wincing in pain.

Once they were a fair distance from the other animals she let go. "I wonder," she mused as the crowd behind them dejectedly dispersed, "exactly what did that bug-eyed delivery dog mean by 'snafu'?"

"I don't rightly know, Captain," Jeremiah said, rubbing his ear. "Maybe that old cat who gave you all that trouble is sick in bed. Oo! I do hope she gets better soon." Blackpaw thumped him on the head, and they continued into town.

Good-Bye Orphanage, Hello Pancakes

Boomish stood at the bow of the *Tasty Pudding*, tapping his foot impatiently as he glanced from Desdemona to Judge Oddkins. Desdemona sat at the rudder, guiding the dory out of Briarberry Harbor while Judge Oddkins secured the sail.

"So, Desdemousa," Boomish said, "*now* can you tell me where we're going, and why you couldn't tell me at the orphanage, and what is in that bag, and what else did I win?"

"It's Desde*mona*," she answered, her whiskers twitching in agitation as she studied the cat. "And I'll explain everything. But why do you think you've won something?"

"Well," he began, ticking items off on his paw. "First, I won a free trip out of the orphanage. Second, I won a new home. That's where you two are taking me, right? What is it, a castle? Crivvens, I've won a castle!" His eyes sparkled as he continued. "I knew I was special, but I didn't know I was a prince. No, not a prince, a king! King Boomish of Briarberry. Hail to the King!"

"My, my, my," chuckled the Judge as he sat down. "It seems you have some explaining to do, Desdemona."

"Master Boomish, listen to me," Desdemona said. "There was no contest."

"Then I don't get it." Boomish blinked. "Why did I get to leave the orphanage?"

The mouse glanced at her carpetbag lying on the bench next to Judge Oddkins. No matter what she thought of him, Boomish was the chosen one. Taking a breath, she said, "What Judge Oddkins and I told you back at Dismal Manor is true. My name is Desdemona, and I am taking you with me. But what I couldn't say is that I was sent to locate and retrieve the next Master Sweet Smith of the Lemon Meringue Islands." Boomish froze, a blank stare on his face. Desdemona and Judge Oddkins exchanged worried glances. "Master Boomish, did you hear what I said?" she asked. "You're the next Saint of Sweets." Boomish didn't move.

"The new Guardian of the Lemon Meringue Islands, my boy," added Judge Oddkins, smiling and nodding.

Slowly, everything around Boomish came back into focus. "So I *am* a king," he said, his face melting into a smile. "No. I'm better than a regular king. Crivvens!" he exclaimed. He leapt onto the bow of the boat, threw out his arms, and bellowed, "I'M THE KING OF DESSERTS!"

Scowling, Desdemona tromped over and pulled Boomish off the bow. "Master Boomish, this is no time for celebration," she scolded, waving a paw in his face. "The Lemon Meringues are in a perilous position—fluffles are falling as we speak, and I must get you and the pan back to the islands as quickly as I can."

"Pan?" Boomish asked. "What pan?"

Desdemona opened the carpetbag and pulled out the now quiet, pan. "This," she said, holding it out to Boomish, "is the magic pancake pan of the Lemon Meringue Islands. One of its most important tasks is to protect the islands, which it can't do when it's not there. But it has other uses as well."

Boomish took the pan from Desdemona and turned it this way and that. He thwacked it with a claw then frowned at the dull tonking sound it made. "Hey," he said. "This pan looks exactly like the ones I used to scrub at the orphanage. Wait a minute. Are you two pulling my paw? Did Magnus put you up to this?"

"Hmm," said Desdemona. "I'm beginning to think listening isn't one of your strong suits. Perhaps a demonstration is in order." She turned toward the badger. "Judge, would you like some pancakes?"

"Yes, yes, indeed. I'm quite starved. Could eat a whale, don't you know," the judge said.

"Pancakes?" Boomish exclaimed. "Crivvens! I'll take two dozen, please." He made grabby motions with his paws as he looked around the boat. "Hey, wait a minute. You two *are* pulling my paw. I don't see any pancakes, and I don't see any Manzipan Gondoliers either."

"Judge Oddkins," Desdemona said, ignoring Boomish, "would you be so kind as to fetch some plates?"

"Yes, yes. Certainly, Desdemona," the judge replied. He disappeared below decks and emerged moments later carrying three plates and a jug of maple syrup. He set down the syrup, handed one plate to Desdemona, and held the other two like catcher's mitts, one in each paw.

"Now, Master Boomish," Desdemona said, "hold out the pan and repeat after me if you please. 'Crick-a-pin, toss-o-tam, here upon my magic pan.'"

Boomish snorted. "Really, Desdemousa. That is just too silly."

"It's Desdemona, and if you want pancakes, you will repeat after me."

"OK, OK. Sheesh." Boomish rolled his eyes, and holding the pan with a weak wrist mumbled, "Crick-a-pin, toss-o-tam, here upon my magic pan."

"Flip-o-fluff, enchant-ee-bakes. Time to munch on pan-ee-cakes."

"Flip-o-fluff, enchant-ee-bakes. Time to munch on pan-ee-cakes," Boomish repeated. Instantly, piping hot pancakes flew from the pan. Judge Oddkins and Desdemona held out their plates, catching the morsels left and right as Boomish stood dumbfounded.

"All right, Master Boomish. That looks like quite enough. Turn the pan over if you please," Desdemona said once the plates were piled high with the fluffy discs. Boomish stood frozen in place, a glazed look in his eyes as the pancakes continued to fly through the air, peppering Desdemona and Judge Oddkins. "Boomish!" shouted Desdemona.

"Huh? Oh!" Coming out of his trance, Boomish turned over the pan, and the flow of pancakes stopped. Desdemona poured a generous helping of syrup onto the plates, and she and Judge Oddkins dug in.

"Absolutely delicious," the judge gushed after swallowing his first bite. "The pan certainly hasn't lost any of its spark."

Boomish picked up a pancake and took a bite. "Mmmm." His eyes bulged as he shoved the rest of the treat into his mouth. "Ths r th best thngs Iv evr eatn!"

"And the pan will make as many as you please," Desdemona said.

"Mmm! Mmmm!" Boomish garbled, his cheeks stretched like a chipmunk's. Judge Oddkins and Desdemona shook their heads as Boomish ate with gusto. When he finished the last crumb, he held up his plate and licked it clean. After a large burp, the cat turned his syrup-coated face to Desdemona. "This is even better than I thought," he said. "First, I get to leave the orphanage. Then, I'm the King of Desserts, and now I find out I've got a magic pancake pan!"

"Yes, and speaking of the pan," Desdemona said, "you do understand how precious it is, don't you? And that you and you alone are responsible for its safe return to the Lemon Meringue Islands?"

"Crivvens," Boomish said, jumping to his feet. For a moment the mouse's spirits rose; Boomish finally grasped the seriousness of his new position. But her hopes were dashed when Boomish said, "We've got to go back to the orphanage and tell everyone who I am. Wait till Magnus hears about this! He's going to—ouch!" he yelped, his paw to his cheek. "What was that for?"

Desdemona dropped the whisker she'd yanked from Boomish's muzzle onto the deck. "Master Boomish!" she said. "Haven't you heard a word I've said? Who you are and where we're going must be kept a secret. The fate of the Lemon Meringue Islands depends on it!"

"Yes, yes," Judge Oddkins chimed in. "We can't let the riffraff know now, can we? All very wink, wink, hush, hush, don't you know?"

"You mean I can't tell *anyone*?" Boomish's mouth dropped open. "But that's—what's the point of being famous if nobody knows who you are?" He crossed his arms and glared at Desdemona, then Judge Oddkins, then Desdemona again.

Desdemona straightened her babushka, which had gone askew during her rant, and tried to calm down. "Don't you see?" she said, looking steadily into his eyes. "Being the Master Sweet Smith isn't about being famous. It's about bringing joy and happiness to those who will never know your name. A true Master Smith realizes that *that* is the sweetest dessert anyone could ever eat. Do you understand?" She paused for a moment, hoping against hope that her words had sunk in. Boomish seemed to be thinking, but about what she couldn't tell. Finally she shook her head. "Well, we'd best make plans for the night's sail."

"You're going to sail at night?" Boomish asked. "Why?"

"Not me. We," she said, circling her paw at the three of them. "We must keep sailing night and day because, as I did mention once or twice, time is of the essence!"

She directed Boomish to the stern, where Judge Oddkins gave him a quick tutorial on how to sail. Boomish clutched the tiller and excitedly yanked it to and fro until Desdemona sternly ordered him to hold it steady. After that, his enthusiasm quickly waned, and he slouched as Judge Oddkins sat next to him, enjoying the sunset. Meanwhile, Desdemona checked the wind and adjusted the sails.

"Um, Judge Oddkins?" Boomish said after a while.

"Yes, my boy?" the Judge said, smiling warmly.

"Do you really think it's a good idea for *me* to be sailing the boat at night? All alone?"

Desdemona turned from her work and raised an eyebrow at Boomish while Judge Oddkins scratched his head. "Well, I...what do you mean?" he said.

"I'm the next King of All Things Yummy, after all," Boomish continued. "Precious cargo. What if something were to happen to me? Wouldn't it be safer for me to be down below?"

Desdemona's face darkened while Judge Oddkins blinked confusedly. "Well I..."

"I mean, is that really wise?"

"Master Boomish," Desdemona snapped, "you will stop pestering poor Judge Oddkins and sail this boat without complaint. And you will take the second shift as planned." She turned and stomped down the stairs.

"Have fun explaining tomorrow why the eyes of the new king are all puffy!" Boomish called after her.

Sometime after midnight, Desdemona looked up at the stars to check her course. Satisfied that the *Pudding* was on track, she tied up the tiller and climbed down to the sleeping cabin.

Inside was warm and dark. The deep breathing of Judge Oddkins and Boomish's gentle snoring filled the room as Desdemona tiptoed over to the bunks and nudged Boomish with her paw. "Hmmm...Wha?" he mumbled. "Are we there yet? Have we reached the islands?"

"No, Master Boomish," she whispered so as not to wake Judge Oddkins. "I came to tell you it's your turn."

"My what?" He opened one eye. "Oh. Right," he said sourly, as the reason for Desdemona's prodding came back to him. He pulled the covers over his head.

Desdemona yanked them back down. "Come along now," she urged. "We can't leave the rudder unattended."

"All right," Boomish huffed. "I'm going." He dragged himself out of his bunk and slumped to the stairs as Desdemona took off her babushka and climbed into her bed.

"Remember to fetch me before first light so I can check our course," she said with a yawn. A moment later she was fast asleep.

Boomish grumbled as he climbed the stairs and stepped out onto the deck. Ambling over to the stern, he untied the tiller and began to sail, a sour look on his face. "This is a fine way to treat the new Ruler of the Lemon Meringues," he groused, his chin on a paw. He yawned and looked toward the east. "Dawn sure is taking a long time to get here." Restlessly, he drummed a paw on the railing. Moments later a gentle breeze blew across his fur. "Jeesh, it's freezing out here!" he said with a shiver. "And Desdemona and Judge Oddkins are all warm and cozy in their bunks."

Boomish looked down at the rope that was used to secure the rudder. "Now that seems like a waste of a perfectly good rope," he said, picking up its loose end and swinging it back and forth. "I don't see why I can't take a tiny catnap while this rope does what it did before perfectly well." Boomish glanced around to make sure no one was coming, then he tied up the tiller and tiptoed across the deck.

Silently, he padded down the stairs, climbed into his bunk, and snuggled under the covers smiling contentedly. "Next stop, Lemon Meringue Islands," he whispered, and drifted off to sleep.

The next morning, a dusty ray of sunlight shone through a porthole and landed on Desdemona's face. Squinting, she lifted a paw to block the beam and slowly opened her eyes. Across the cabin, Judge Oddkins and Boomish were also stirring. The judge put on his spectacles while Boomish looked over at Desdemona and smiled sleepily.

"Good morning, Desdemona," he said with a yawn. "Are we there yet?"

"Good morning, Master Boomish. Actually I—Master Boomish?" she exclaimed, sitting bolt upright. "Who's minding the rudder?"

"Who's what?" Boomish said. "Oh! Um..."

"How long have you been sleeping?" Desdemona demanded, hopping out of bed and pulling on her babushka while Judge Oddkins looked on in concern.

Boomish thought for a moment. "Well..."

"Oh, for the love of Betsy," Desdemona exclaimed. She scurried up the steps and shoved open the hatch.

"EEEK!" she screeched. "Master Boomish, get up here on the double!"

"OK, OK. I'm coming," he said, climbing the steps with Judge Oddkins at his heels. The two animals stepped onto the deck and started toward the bow, where Desdemona was standing with her eyes bulging and her hands on her hips. Boomish and Judge Oddkins were just passing the mast when the boat tilted forward, sending them somersaulting into the mouse.

"Whoa! The sea's a little bumpy, I see," said Boomish as he untangled himself.

"Oh, it's more than bumpy," she replied as she stood up and brushed herself off. "Take a look over the side, if you please."

Judge Oddkins straightened up, and he and Boomish looked over the rail. Boomish winced. "Oh my," Judge Oddkins gasped in dismay. "My, my, my!"

After Boomish had left the *Pudding* to sail herself, she'd drifted off course and sailed onto a shallow rock, becoming jammed. Then the tide had gone out, and the boat was left teeter tottering on the rock, high and dry.

"Master Boomish, how could you?" Desdemona squeaked.

"Um, well, I..." Boomish looked off across the water, his forehead wrinkled in thought. Suddenly, his face brightened as he spotted a speck of land in the distance.

"What are we going to do now?" Desdemona wailed. "Stranded in the middle of the ocean, our ship hopelessly stuck."

"Ahem," Boomish interrupted. "Actually, Desdemona, you should be thanking me."

"Now, now, my boy—" Judge Oddkins warned, but Desdemona cut him off.

"Thanking you?" she said, looking as if smoke was about to pour from her ears. "What in Betsy's name for?"

Boomish pointed triumphantly at what looked like a pile of rocks off the bow. "You see, Desdemona?" he said. "There they are. The Lemon Meringue Islands!" Desdemona and the Judge followed his paw with their eyes. Desdemona moaned and buried her face in her paws. Judge Oddkins simply shook his head. "What?" Boomish asked.

Before they could answer, a strange voice called out, "Hello! Hello up-a there!" The three animals looked back over the side of the *Pudding*. Floating below them was a barnacle-encrusted fishing boat manned by ferrets.

"Oh, ahoy there," said Desdemona. "It seems we've had a bit of an accident."

The ferrets chuckled. "We can-a see that!" their captain called, thoroughly entertained by the spectacle he and his crew had come across.

"Yes, well," she said, laughing stiffly, "could you please tell us where we are?"

"Si! Thatsa easy one! You is-a offa the coast of Heckler's Hunch. My boys and I, we are justa heading in. Maybe you could use a lift, no?"

The first mate poked his captain in the ribs and said, "Looksa like they already got one." The crew laughed uproariously.

Boomish scowled.

"Heckler's Hunch," Desdemona moaned. "Betsy preserve us. Why did it have to be Heckler's Hunch?"

Judge Oddkins patted Desdemona's paw reassuringly and called to the captain, "Yes, yes, very good! I believe we'll take you up on your kind offer. Thank you. If you'll wait one moment, we'll gather our things."

"Thatsa fine," the captain called back over his crew's dying laughter.

As the judge waddled down the stairs to retrieve the pan, Desdemona turned on Boomish. "Now you listen to me, Master Boomish. Because of you, we've landed in the worst, most dangerous town in all the Bewhiskered Lands."

"Really?" Boomish scratched his head, squinting at the lump of land.

"So the pan is to remain hidden at all times," she hissed.

"OK. Sheesh!"

"And not a whisper about who you are or where we're going. Do you understand?" she said, poking him in the belly after each word.

"Jeez, Desdemona," Boomish said, rubbing his stomach. "I know I made a little boo-boo, but don't you think you're being a bit of a worrywart?"

"A little boo-boo?" the mouse practically shrieked. "You destroyed the *Pudding*, cost us precious time that we can ill afford to lose, and have landed us in the place most likely to derail our mission. That is hardly what I would call 'a little boo-boo'!"

"Well, when you put it that way," Boomish muttered, "I guess you shouldn't be thanking me."

Desdemona clenched her fists as Judge Oddkins emerged with the carpetbag. "Ready to disembark?" he said, handing it to Boomish. Making a face like he'd just smelled garbage,

Boomish started to ask for something else to carry the pan in, but Desdemona's face changed his mind.

A subdued Boomish, an aggravated Desdemona, and a smiling Judge Oddkins abandoned the *Pudding* and sailed with the ferrets toward Heckler's Hunch.

What's The Big Idea?

Boomish received quite an earful from Desdemona on the ride to Heckler's Hunch, and by the time the fishing boat pulled into the harbor, he was beginning to think he'd never have any fun being the new Master Sweet Smith.

After the ferrets lassoed their ship to one of the rotted piers, Boomish, Desdemona, and Judge Oddkins disembarked, then turned to say their good-byes. "Thank you so much for the ride, Captain," Desdemona said.

"No problema!" boomed the captain.

"Yes, yes. Quite helpful indeed," Judge Oddkins chimed in.

"Good-bye," mumbled Boomish.

Once they were out of earshot of the ferrets, Desdemona and Judge Oddkins stopped to discuss their next course of action. Desdemona insisted on hiring their own boat as their mission was such a sensitive one. But the judge pointed out a larger ship would get them to the Lemon Meringues much faster.

Bored by their conversation, Boomish looked around and spotted a group of girls standing in a semicircle farther down the dock. Swinging the bag at his side, he sauntered over and waited expectantly for the girls to notice him. They paid no attention. They were too busy giggling at something in front of them. Wondering what could possibly be so captivating, Boomish peeked over their heads. Leaning over and coiling a heavy rope was a strapping young dog with a rich brown coat, pointed black-tipped ears, and perfect teeth. Boomish scowled. "Ahh," the girls sighed as the dog's muscles rippled under his shiny fur.

Peevishly, Boomish pushed his way front and center and coughed, "Ahem."

Hefting the rope over his shoulder, the dog straightened up, his head stopping a good three feet above everyone else's. He studied the cat for a moment, taking note of Boomish's sour expression and Desdemona's flowery carpetbag. "Nice purse," he said.

The girls tittered. Boomish blushed and dropped the bag behind him as he glared at the dog. But before he could utter a comeback, a gravelly voice rang out from across the pier. "Hello! Is that Desdemona I see?"

Hop-stepping over the occasional hole toward Desdemona and Judge Oddkins was a stout old dog with graying fur. Around his expansive waist hung a green and red tartan kilt. Matching woolen socks with shiny gold tassels covered his knees, and topping off the look was a balmoral with a bright red pom pom.

Curious, Boomish wandered over while Desdemona greeted the dog warmly. "Wizzencoots!" she said. "I can scarcely believe it. What are you doing in Heckler's Hunch of all places?"

"Why, me grandson an' I sailed into port a year ago teu attend teu some much needed repairs an', well," Wizzencoots laughed embarrassedly, "it took a bit o' time, but she's joost about there." He pointed down the pier at a weathered, three-masted caravel, the name *Flying Grizzella* in peeling paint on the hull.

Desdemona's face lit up at the sight of Wizzencoots's ship. It seemed the perfect solution to their predicament. "So she's ready to sail?" she said.

"Aye," Wizzencoots's voice wavered a bit. "She joost needs a coat o' paint an' the crows booted out o' the crow's nest."

While Desdemona squinted at the actual nest on top of the *Grizzella*'s mast, the young dog strode up, his tail wagging. The giggling girls trailed after him. The dog didn't seem to notice. Boomish made a face. "Well, here's ol' Danny Boy noo," Wizzencoots said, patting the dog on the back, which was as high as he could reach. "Desdemona, this is me grandson, Dan. Danny, meet Desdemona an'..." He stopped and furrowed two furry, caterpillar-like eyebrows at Boomish and Judge Oddkins.

"Goodness me. Where are my manners?" Desdemona said, making the introductions.

"Bless my barnacles! Nae the famous Judge Oddkins himself?" Wizzencoots nearly choked.

"Now, now, now. If I was well known, it was quite some time ago," said the Judge.

"Pleased to meet you, Judge Oddkins," Dan said, shaking the judge's paw. "And mighty pleased to meet you both," he said to Boomish and Desdemona. Boomish pretended to study one of the holes in the pier.

"Wizzencoots, I had no idea you had such a handsome grandson," Desdemona said. Boomish bristled.

"Aye," Wizzencoots said. "Boot Danny here is nae joost another pretty face. Why, Danny's smart as a whip. Never a grade below an A. Can yeu believe it?"

"Oh, Gramps," Dan said.

"Nae oonly that," Wizzencoots continued, "Danny won farst place in the Spring Hoedown." He hopped about, demonstrating some of Dan's winning steps. Desdemona, Judge Oddkins, and the girls clapped. Boomish fake smiled then sulked. "An' joost last week Danny won the Rowboat Regatta!"

Desdemona, Judge Oddkins, and the girls *oohed* and *ahhed*. Boomish burned with jealousy. "Gramps, enough," Dan begged.

"Och, all right." Wizzencoots punched Dan affectionately on the forearm, then studied Desdemona and company. "Besides," he said, "it's about time I asked Desdemona here what brings her teu this viper's den."

"Excellent question, Wizzencoots," Desdemona replied. "And one I would love to explain as soon as possible. Why don't we head to the Merry Spinster and discuss it over dinner? My treat."

"Never tarn down a free meal. That's what I always say," Wizzencoots chuckled. "I'll go freshen up a bit, an' I'll meet yeu there!"

Wizzencoots hurried off to the *Grizzella* while Dan went back to work, the group of girls in tow. Boomish shot Dan's retreating back a last dirty look, then slumped after Desdemona and Judge Oddkins.

As they walked, the mouse nodded toward three small piglets with pleading eyes sitting on the edge of the dock. The smallest one held a sign that read, "Will Work for Cupcakes." Judge Oddkins shook his head sadly. Desdemona poked Boomish in the ribs. "You see Master Boomish? Just another sign of the troubles that have started and will keep getting worse until—" She stopped suddenly, gaping at Boomish's empty paws. "Where is the carpetbag?" she said.

Boomish held out his paws, looking at them in surprise. "Umm..." He turned around and spotted it on the dock among the skirts of gigging girls watching Dan roll a barrel across the dock. "It's right over there," he said, as if he'd left it there on purpose.

"Well, you'd best run and fetch it, then," the mouse said, looking as though she'd like to pull all his whiskers out at once.

Jealously eyeing the girls, Boomish nodded his head. "Right away, Desdemona. You and Judge Oddkins go on ahead, and I'll meet you at the Happy Hag."

"It's the Merry Spinster!" Desdemona said. "And if you expect me to let you wander around this den of vermin when you've just misplaced the pan and—"

"Now, now, Desdemona," Judge Oddkins said. "We must consider the lad's new position. The time for him to learn responsibility is now, don't you think?"

"That's right," Boomish said, one eye on the girls who were pointing at Dan while he hoisted the barrel onto a boat. "How am I going to learn respons—what the judge said if you don't give me a chance?"

"Well..." Desdemona stared at him long and hard while Boomish danced from foot to foot impatiently. "I suppose Judge Oddkins is right. But Master Boomish, remember what I said. Meet us at the Merry Spinster forthwith. Understand? No tomfoolery!"

Boomish tore his eyes away from Dan and the girls, held up a paw, and said, "Aye, aye, captain."

Desdemona was not amused. She pursed her lips doubtfully while Judge Oddkins gave Boomish directions to the inn. "Straight into town and turn right at the barber shop," the judge repeated until Boomish was finally able to say it back correctly.

Boomish waited until Desdemona and Judge Oddkins were a good way down the dock, then puffing out his chest, he approached the group once more. Dan had finished moving the barrels and was sitting on a crate polishing a brass bell. Boomish picked up the bag and, keeping it tucked behind his back, walked up to Dan and pointed at the bell with his free paw.

"You missed a spot," he told the dog.

Dan didn't even look up. "Not likely," he said. The girls giggled. Boomish opened his mouth but couldn't think of a reply. He paced back and forth, wracking his brains for a way to impress the others. Sighing heavily, Dan stopped polishing. "Forget something?" he said, nodding at the bag sticking out from behind Boomish.

The girls tittered, and Boomish bristled. "Maybe I did," he said. "But for your information, in this bag are some very important papers for Judge Oddkins's upcoming case, and I'm helping him." The girls *oohed* in awe.

"That's interesting," said Dan blandly.

"Oh, it's more than interesting. It's murder!" Boomish hissed. The girls squealed and hugged one another.

"A murder case?" Dan said, raising an eyebrow. "Really? Well that *is* more than interesting seeing as how the judge hasn't sat on the bench in at least ten years." Boomish slumped as Dan rubbed his chin. "As a matter of fact," he continued, "if I recollect correctly, the last thing Judge Oddkins officiated was the annual pie-eating contest, although those can be pretty dangerous, I hear."

The girls giggled, and Boomish's ears turned crimson. "Well, I just said all that because I'm not supposed to tell what I'm really doing here."

"Uh huh," Dan said, back to polishing his bell.

"That's right. I'm actually here on a secret voyage!" The girls *oohed* and *ahhed*.

"Secret voyage, huh?" Dan said to his bell. "Impressive. Where to?"

The girls looked expectantly at Boomish. "To the...to the...oooh!" he said. "I'm not allowed to tell!"

"I guess that's about as secret as you can get," Dan said. The girls giggled, and Boomish stood clenching his paws while Dan finished the bell and began loading some crates onto a boat. The girls watched him with goo-goo eyes.

"But you don't understand," Boomish cried, "I'm important. Really, really important!" No one paid any attention, except for one small girl bunny whose ears perked up.

"My granny says I'm important too," she said, smiling up at Boomish.

"Yeah, but I'm *stupendalously* important," Boomish said, glaring at Dan and the girls.

"Granny says it's my birthday tomorrow, and we always have pancakes," the bunny said, her eyes sparkling.

"That's nice," Boomish mumbled, thinking there should be a law against ignoring the King of Desserts.

"But this year we might not because there aren't any pancakes," she said, her ears drooping. Boomish finally heard the word "pancakes" and perked up as an idea began to take shape.

"So, I asked Granny," the bunny continued, tears welling up in her eyes, "'Where did all the pancakes go?'"

Boomish's face lit up as the plan came together. "You want pancakes?" he asked. The bunny nodded hopefully. "Well, that's easy!" he said. "I can make you pancakes." The bunny squealed and hopped excitedly. "In fact," Boomish added, shooting a look at Dan and the girls, "I can make pancakes for everybody." Scrambling to the top of a nearby pile of crates he called out, "Attention! Attention everyone! Who wants pancakes?"

The girls and a few fishermen looked up. The piglets perked their ears and trotted over. Dan put down the crate he was moving. "What did you say?" he said.

"I said," Boomish shot back, "'Who wants pancakes?'"

"I do!" One of the fishermen, a beaver with a protruding belly, raised his paw. The piglets nodded vigorously.

Dan gaped at Boomish in disbelief. "I realize you're new in town, so let me fill you in a little. Everyone in Heckler's Hunch knows the Marzipan Grenadiers haven't delivered anything but biscuits lately. So unless you've got a secret supply of pancakes in that bag"—he pointed at the carpetbag—"you're out of luck."

"You're the one who's out of luck, my mistooken friend," Boomish muttered under his breath. By now, a large crowd had gathered around the pile of crates as more townsfolk wandered over to see what all the fuss was about.

Basking in all the attention, Boomish shot Dan a triumphant look and cried, "Hear ye, hear ye! I, Boomish of Briarberry, do hereby give public notice of a great and stupendelous pancake breakfast in honor of, um..." He glanced down at the bunny. "What's your name?" he said.

"Geraldine!" she squealed.

"...in honor of Geraldine's birthday, at the Merry Spinster tomorrow morning at eight o'clock sharp!" The crowd cheered. The "Will Work for Cupcakes" sign flew into the air. Geraldine hopped up and down, and the giggling girls made extra gooey goo-goo eyes at Boomish.

Dan frowned. "Let me get this straight," he said. "You're going to provide pancakes for, let me see..."—he counted with his paw—"over fifty critters? Now just how do you plan to pull that off?"

"Don't you worry your big dog head about that," Boomish gloated. "You just make sure you show up tomorrow. Oh, and don't forget your manners!"

The excited crowd began chanting, "Pancakes! Pancakes!" Boomish did a few fancy dance steps, then took a bow and hopped onto the dock. The crowd swarmed around him as he made his way toward town. A fisherman shook his paw. Townsfolk patted him on the back. The giggling girls trailed after him, and Geraldine hugged herself with joy. Dan watched him go, shook his head, and walked away.

The Not-So-Merry Spinster

After a few wrong turns down some dark alleyways, Boomish burst into the Merry Spinster like he was walking on air. Lost in visions of the morrow's triumphant pancake breakfast, he scarcely noticed the cracked wood floors, dirt-caked windows, and unsavory characters loitering in the dark corners of the inn.

When he reached the lopsided doorway of the common room, he scanned the sea of gruff and grizzled faces for Desdemona or Judge Oddkins. Spotting the tips of the badger's ears peeking over the back of a booth, he headed over, the bag held proudly at his side.

A group of fishermen waved at him from the bar. One of them held up a glass of watered down root beer and called, "See you tomorrow, Bluefish!"

Boomish pointed to himself as if to ask, "Me?" then shook his paws in false modesty.

He reached the booth, and as he scooted in next to Wizzencoots, he caught sight of a muskrat in a farmer's hat sitting in the booth behind him. Pulling the carpetbag in next to him, and avoiding Desdemona's questioning stare, he glanced hungrily at the plates on the table. "Ah, Master Boomish," Judge Oddkins said. "You're just in time." He looked down at his food. "Well now, where to start?" he mused, poking at it with a fork. "Everything looks so...gray."

"Yes, well, let's make the best of it," Desdemona said, not questioning Boomish about his tardiness for the moment. "Tomorrow we set sail, and before you know it, we'll be having much better fare."

Wizzencoots gulped down a forkful of food and smacked his lips. "Ah, joost what the doctor ordered." He elbowed Boomish and said, "Would yeu mind passin' me the chutney there, laddie?" Boomish slid over a jar filled with giggly, green goo, and Wizzencoots scooped a heaping spoonful of it onto his plate.

Across from them, an enormous bull leaned back so a sullen-looking serving pig in a frilly apron could pick up his plate. She dropped it onto her tray and turned to go. "Excuse me," said the bull, "could you please tell me what you have for dessert?" Without a word, the pig reached into her apron pocket, pulled out a biscuit, and slammed it down on the table.

Wizzencoots chuckled as the bull stared at the smushed biscuit in dismay. "Must be from out o' town or he'd have known better," the old dog said. "Desserts are mighty hard to come by lately." Desdemona and Judge Oddkins exchanged worried glances. Wizzencoots took a big swallow from his mug and made a prune face. "Blasted barnacles!" he spat. "There's nae I hate more than watered down root beer." He wiped his tongue on his napkin then said, "Speakin' of settin' sail on the morrow, what I dinnae know señorita, is just where yeu're wantin' teu go."

Desdemona leveled her gaze at the old dog as he shoved another forkful of food into his mouth. "Well," she said. "I was hoping we'd be on our way without divulging our secret to anyone. But as you're a trusted friend with a fast ship, it seems that fate has other plans." Wizzencoots swallowed his food as Desemona leaned forward and whispered, "We're going to the Lemon Meringue Islands."

"The Lemon Meringue *ack*!" the old dog choked.

Desdemona frantically waved her paws. "Yes, yes. But please, Wizzencoots," she hissed. "Keep your voice down!" Judge Oddkins glanced at the other diners, but none of them seemed to have heard.

In the next booth, however, Jeremiah sat like a statue, foam dripping from his whiskers as he listened intently.

"Well noo, señorita," Wizzencoots said, eyeing Desdemona appraisingly, "it must be goin' on fifteen years since we sailed together making deliveries far ol' man Frominoff. Looks like yeu've been moving in some mighty different circles since then." Desdemona shrugged, and Judge Oddkins cleared his throat uncomfortably. But Boomish squirmed in his seat, waiting impatiently for Desdemona to get to the best and most important part. Wizzencoots scratched his chin and studied Desdemona's poker face. "Tell me," he said. "What business do yeu have at the islands? Last time I checked, it was strictly off limits teu civilians."

Desdemona was about to answer when Boomish burst out, "Yes, but the old Queen of Desserts has died, and I'm the new King!"

"Boomish!" Desdemona exploded.

"And," he continued, "I have a magic pancake pan, too!" A *thud* sounded from nearby, and Judge Oddkins and Wizzencoots hastily looked around. Desdemona yanked out a pawful of Boomish's whiskers. "Yeow! Hey! What was that for?" Boomish cried out. Desdemona was too furious to speak.

In the next booth, Jeremiah quietly climbed off the floor and back onto his bench, then took off his hat so he could hear better.

Not seeing anything suspicious, Wizzencoots turned his attention back to the news he'd just heard. "Well noo, that explains it!" he said, slapping his knee. "Yeu'd have a better chance of meetin' an honest pirate than gettin' a piece of pumpkin pie around here lately."

"Hey!" came a hurt-sounding voice from the next booth.

The group looked around, then Desdemona continued, "So as you can see, Wizzencoots, you seem to be the ingredient we need to finish this recipe. Will you help us?"

Wizzencoots sat in thought for a moment. "I'll do it," he boomed, whacking a paw on the table. "Nae tarn down a friend in need, I always say. Besides," he said, glancing around the room, "if these hooligans go without dessert mooch longer, there's no tellin' who might get tarred an' feathered. Athoo," he added, scratching an ear, "the mood in this place tonight is almost cheery, though I cannae say why."

A table of animals waved at Boomish to get his attention, then rubbed their stomachs and gave him the thumbs up. Boomish stuck up his two thumbs under the table so Desdemona wouldn't notice, then turned his attention back to the conversation.

"And I'll be bringin' Danny boy along, of course," Wizzencoots was saying. "Cannae sail the *Grizzella* without him."

"Dan, shman!" Boomish muttered under his breath.

"Of course," Desdemona said. "And thank you, Wizzencoots. You're a real lifesaver! We'll meet you on the docks first thing in the morning."

"Och! Well noo, that's quick, isn't it. Aye, I'll be ready."

Desdemona raised her glass. "To success."

Boomish, Wizzencoots, and Judge Oddkins clinked their mugs against hers. "To success!" they chorused.

In the next booth, Jeremiah raised his glass and grinned. "Success indeed," he said, his eyes round as marbles. Taking a last sip from his mug, he threw on his hat, and hurried out of the inn.

A Tasty Tidbit

Jeremiah didn't stop running until he reached the *Pink Princess*, aka, the *Cat O' Nine Tails*. He signaled the pirate on duty and gasped for air while the gangplank was slid into place. As soon as it touched down, Jeremiah hurried across and waddled as fast as he could to the captain's cabin.

He slipped through the open door and waited, dancing impatiently while the boatswain, a nervous looking skunk, finished making his report. "I told Stumpy to get the supplies, but I guess he heard 'surprise,' and so that's why the hold is full o' balloons, Cap'n," he was saying. The boatswain gulped nervously as this news was met with silence and a particularly nasty stare from the captain. But Blackpaw had only been half listening. Her trip into town that morning had been a disaster. All her usual contacts were completely out of sweets, and she'd returned to the ship empty-pawed.

She didn't know what was going on. She glared into space until Jeremiah's dancing and heavy breathing caught her attention. Waving the skunk away she said shortly, "What is it, Jeremiah?"

"Oh, what indeed! What indeed! Ol' Jerry's really gone and done it this time. Yes I have, Captain!" Jeremiah panted.

"Maybe we should calm ourselves, and then you can tell me what you've gone and done," Blackpaw snapped.

"Right, Captain," Jeremiah said, taking a deep breath and exhaling. "Well, remember when you told me to head over to the Merry Spinster and keep my ears open for any tidbits?"

Blackpaw spun a gold coin on her desk and eyed him impatiently. "Quickly please, Jeremiah."

"Uh, yes, Captain!" he stammered. "Straight away is the best way, and anyway, that's what I always say, so, as for today, let me just say—" Blackpaw flicked the coin, hitting Jeremiah on the nose. "Ouch!" he said.

"You have five seconds, Jeremiah. Five..." she began to count down.

"Aye, aye, Captain," Jeremiah said, flustered. "Well, I was havin' some weak ginger ale—"

"Four..."

"Well, you know how I hate weak ginger ale, and there were—"

"Three..."

"...were critters in the next booth," he continued frantically, "and they were—"

"Two..."

He wrung his paws together. "They were talking about the—the—" Realizing he was almost out of time, he slapped a paw over his mouth and ran over to the map. Frantically, he pointed to the Lemon Meringue Islands.

Blackpaw's gaze followed the paw, and her eyes grew round. "One."

Something Whiskered This Way Comes

Back at the Merry Spinster, Wizzencoots was taking his leave. "Danny an' I'll be warkin' the better part o' the night gettin' the ship in shipshape, so I'd best be off," he said, chuckling at his own joke. "Get it?" he said. "Ship in shipshape?" When no one laughed, he waved them off and headed out the door.

"My, my," Judge Oddkins sputtered. "I completely forgot to ask Wizzencoots about the provisions. I'll be right back," he said and hurried off.

As he left, Mildred, the sullen serving pig, came to the table carrying half the items on the menu that a ravenous Boomish had ordered. "Speaking of tomorrow," Boomish said as he scooped up a pawful of mashed peas, "just what time is 'first thing'?"

"Well…" said Desdemona, sliding a fork over to Boomish. Boomish pursed his lips, but wanting to get on Desdemona's good side, he took the fork and began eating as the mouse went over the particulars.

"...so with a bit of luck we should be able to make our final destination by Tuesday," she concluded.

Boomish, who hadn't heard one word, said, "So, what I'm hearing from you is that it doesn't really matter what time we leave tomorrow." He shoveled more food into his mouth, and before Desdemona could answer, continued, "In fct, eff we lft at arrund tnn, it wudnt rlly mttr." He swallowed. "Right?"

"Just what is going on, Master Boomish?" Desdemona demanded.

Just then, a pleasant-looking serving pig carrying pitchers of fizzle beer passed by their booth. She glanced at Boomish and did a double take. "'Ello, luv," she said. "Ain't you the bloke who's frowin' the big pancake breakfast tomorrow for Geraldine's bufday?" Boomish grinned. Desdemona's mouth dropped open. "Blimey," the server went on, "I was gob-smacked when I 'eard about it! Imagine, a complete stranger making a little gul's bufday wish come true. Mildred there"— she pointed a pitcher at the pig who scowled in return—"says you're completely gormy. But I fink it's the luvliest fing I ever 'eard. I'm so chuffed I can 'ardly wait!"

"Mollie!" shouted the bartender gruffly. "Cut the chit-chat and hustle your bacon over to table five!"

"Sorry, luv," said the pig. "Got to get back to me work." She flashed Boomish an adoring smile and hurried off. Boomish watched her go, his chest puffed out in pride. Then he saw Desdemona's face. The mouse was glowering at him, waiting for an explanation. Boomish laughed weakly.

"So," Desdemona said with fake lightheartedness, "you promised a little girl you'd throw her a pancake breakfast tomorrow, did you?"

"Well, um…"

"Tell me, Master Boomish," she continued, "just how were you going to explain the sudden appearance of all those pancakes in town?"

Boomish started in surprise at her question, realizing there might be one or two teeny details about his breakfast he hadn't quite worked out. "Hmm…well…um. Oh, I know! It's very simple. Once everyone gets their pancakes, we hop on the *Grizzella* and leave. And the townsfolk will always remember it as the Pancake Miracle!" Boomish grinned and waited for Desdemona to congratulate him on his brilliant idea.

Instead, she shot Boomish a withering look. "I've heard enough," she said, scooting out of the booth. "I'm going up to our room, but you will not be joining me. You are going down to the docks to help Wizzencoots and Dan prepare for tomorrow's departure. And while you're there, ask him if he would be so kind as to provide you with a bunk for the night." Boomish held out his paws in a "What did I do?" gesture. "Oh," she continued, "in addition, I will be taking the pan with me. You have missed your last chance to prove yourself, and it would be irresponsible of me to leave something so important in the paws of someone as foolhardy as you." Swiping the carpetbag off the bench, she turned and stomped off, leaving Boomish alone with his thoughts, which he really didn't like thinking about.

"Boy," he said. "Desdemona really got herself worked up over nothing! Well, almost nothing. Just a little tiny thing, really." He poked at his food. "And just because I wanted to do a kind deed, she's going to make me work all night. And with that know-it-all Dan, too. That big, dumb dummy. Well, if he thinks he's going to boss me around all night, he's sadly mistooken." Boomish was still muttered when Judge Oddkins slid back into the booth.

"Ah, Master Boomish," said the badger. "Still here, I see." He looked around the half-empty dining room. "Where's Desdemona?"

"She went up to bed," Boomish said, still lost in his unhappy thoughts.

"My, my. Did she now?" Judge Oddkins blinked. "Well, it is getting late," he said, with a yawn. "I suppose we should be heading up as well." He waved a paw at Mildred. The sullen pig stomped over, smacked the bill on the table, and plodded away.

Boomish sunk lower in his seat. Dan and the *Grizzella* were moments away. Judge Oddkins dropped some coins down on the table and stood up. "Judge Oddkins, wait,'" Boomish said, grabbing the badger's sleeve.

"My, my. How rude of me," the judge apologized, looking at Boomish's half-full plates. "You're not done with your dinner, are you?"

"No, it's not that," Boomish said. "I um...I forgot to tell you that the inn made a mistake and gave your room to someone else."

"Gave my room away?" Judge Oddkins said, sinking back onto the seat. "Well, well. That's quite unfortunate, isn't it?"

"Yes, it is. Especially since there are no extra beds in the room I'm sharing with Desdemona," Boomish added, clueless as to whether or not this was true.

"My, my," the Judge murmured.

"But don't worry," Boomish said. "There's plenty of room on the *Grizzella*, and Desdemona said you could sleep there."

The badger sat in thought for a moment. "Well, well," he said, standing back up, "if that's the case, the sooner I'm off the better. Goodnight, my boy. I'll see you bright and early in the morning." He gave Boomish a warm smile and padded to the exit, holding the door open for Mollie, who'd finished her shift and was heading home.

Boomish sat at the table trying to finish his dinner, but instead he pushed the food around on his plate. "What is this ookie feeling in my tummy?" he said to himself. "And why am I not happy about not having to slave away like I did back at the orphanage? It almost feels like I might have done something wrong." He rested his paw on his stomach and sulked.

The last fisherman tumbled off his barstool and staggered toward the door. As he passed Boomish, he said, "See you tomorrow, Boomer!" Boomish smiled weakly in return. He picked up a bit of food but then set it back down on his plate.

With a heavy sigh, Boomish started scooching out of his seat, but paused when he heard a *Click click! Click click!* The sound of ladies' shoes came closer until it stopped in front of his booth. Boomish looked up and found himself staring into the face of the most beautiful cat he'd ever seen. She was dressed in a pink satin ball gown with layer upon layer of purple ruffles, and her glove-covered paws nervously fiddled with an enormous, lace-trimmed hat as she glanced shyly down. Boomish had never seen such an adorable pink nose, silky white fur, or sparkly blue eyes. "Pardon me," said the cat, her voice high and sweet. "Is this seat taken?"

"Crivvens!" was the only word Boomish could say.

Blackpaw, for that was who she was, blushed and said, "I do apologize for being so dreadfully forward. It's just that"— she looked around helplessly—"well, Heckler's Hunch does have a rather bad reputation, and you have such kind eyes. I would just feel so much safer sitting with you." She blinked bashfully as she waited for Boomish to speak.

"Ooo!" Boomish cried. "You want to sit here? With me? Oh. Sure! Here, sit down." He jumped up to help her into the booth but tripped and stumbled into her, sending her flying into the booth face first. "Ooo! Ooo!" Boomish exclaimed. "I'm so sorry!" Frantically, he sifted through layers of satin until he found a gloved paw. "Here, let me help you," he said as he tugged. But he pulled too hard and Blackpaw was yanked over onto her side. Boomish attempted to help again, but she waved him off. Pushing herself upright, she removed her lopsided hat and smoothed her dress as Boomish returned to his seat. "Gee, I'm really sorry about that," he said.

"Oh, that's quite all right," Blackpaw said sweetly. "You probably don't know your own strength. You're so manly!" Boomish swelled up like a bullfrog. Blackpaw held out a paw. "My name is Nancy," she said, her voice as light as air. "Nancy

Skipchurch. Charmed, I'm sure." Boomish took the paw and squeezed, gazing adoringly into Blackpaw's blue eyes. The seconds ticked by. "And you are?"

"Who, me?" Boomish started. "Um...my name, uh...oh gosh, my name. Uh, my name is, uh, Boo...Boooo..."

"Booboo?" Blackpaw giggled, her voice like tinkling bells. "Well, that's certainly an interesting name."

"Oh! No, no, no! Not Booboo," Boomish laughed stiffly. "I meant Boomish. Yes, Boomish of Briarberry at your service." He attempted a bow and whacked his head on the table.

"Boomish of Briarberry. Why, it sounds so noble," she gasped. "I'm awfully pleased to meet you, Boomish of Briarberry." Boomish beamed. "Well, Boomish," Blackpaw continued, "I do hope you don't mind my sitting with you. It's just that I'm traveling alone, and well, this really isn't my kind of place, if you know what I mean." She glanced anxiously around at the last two animals left in the room, an old goat asleep at a table and Mildred, who was wiping down the bar.

"Oh, I know what you mean." Boomish nodded gravely. "A lot of shifty characters around here. But don't worry. I'll protect you."

"Oh, that's awfully nice of you," Blackpaw gushed. "Now, if I could just get that server's attention, maybe I could finally feed myself today. She pulled out a lace hankie and waved it weakly at the pig.

Boomish, seeing an opportunity to help the fair maiden in distress, shot to his feet and called, "Attention! Attention please! You there, Madame Pig, the good lady here requires food. Quick! Bring the best you have to offer!"

Mildred stopped wiping, waddled over, and said shortly, "It's half past ten and the kitchen's closed." Then, shooting Boomish a dirty look, she clomped back to the bar.

Blackpaw looked crestfallen. She called after the pig, "Oh, that's OK. It's not your fault, I'm sure. Thanks anyway." Boomish was sure he'd never ever met such a sweet, brave girl. "Well," Blackpaw said, her voice growing weaker by the second, "it looks like I'll have to wait till breakfast. I suppose I should turn in now and try to get some sleep." She sighed sadly. "I only hope I can. You know how hard it can be to sleep on an empty stomach." She flashed Boomish a heartbreaking smile and started to rise.

Boomish's heart sank. "Wait!" he exclaimed, desperately searching for a reason for her to stay. There was only one reason he could think of. "Pancakes!" he choked out.

Blackpaw sat back down. "Excuse me?" She blinked.

"What I mean is," Boomish started again, "you said you were hungry, and I was wondering if you would like some pancakes."

"Pancakes?" Blackpaw said, her eyes lighting up. "Oh, I simply adore pancakes! But stop," she said. "You wouldn't be having a joke on me now, would you?" She placed her paws to her cheeks, blushing embarrassedly. "Well, of course you would. Why, I was told only yesterday that Heckler's Hunch was out of sweets." She shook her head. "My daddy always said I was too trusting." Once again she started to leave.

"No, wait!" Boomish blurted out. "Really, I can make you pancakes right now!" He looked around the pub. Mildred had gone home. Only the goat was still there, snoring away. "Just wait here, and I promise I'll be right back with the most delicious pancakes you've ever had."

"Well, if you're sure it's not too much trouble," Blackpaw said.

"Oh, no," he assured her. "No trouble at all." Hopping out of the booth, he bowed and said, "Till next I see you." Then he turned and raced out of the room.

The second Boomish was out of sight, Blackpaw hitched up her skirts and *click clicked* as fast as she could to an open window. Sticking her head out she hissed, "Jeremiah!"

The muskrat poked his head out of a bush. "Yes, Captain?"

"He's getting the pan," she said gruffly. "Now get to the kitchen and don't come back until it's in your furry paw. And make sure you see and hear everything that lovestruck bumpkin does. I can't use the pan if I don't know how it works."

"Aye, aye, Captain. Right away," said Jeremiah. He tumbled out of the bush and scuttled around the back of the inn while Blackpaw hustled back to her seat.

A minute later, Boomish blew back into the room, the carpetbag in his paw. "Just getting my apron," he said, patting the bag as he ran by. "Don't move. I'll be back with your pancakes in a teensy second."

Breathing heavily, Boomish pushed open the swinging door to the kitchen and poked his head in. "Hello," he said. "Anyone home?" No one was, so he tossed the bag onto the counter and pulled out the pan.

Outside in the alleyway, Jeremiah stood on an empty crate, squinting through a grimy window at the blurry blob that was Boomish. Nervously, he bit a claw as he remembered Blackpaw's orders and decided to risk opening the window.

Carefully, he wedged his claws under the bottom of the window, and holding his breath, lifted it up a few inches and peeked inside.

"Get ready, Nancy, for the best pancakes you've ever had," Boomish was saying as he rubbed his paws together.

As he always did when he was cooking, Boomish put on an apron and a tall white chef's hat. Then he held out the pan and chanted, "Crick-a-pin, toss-o-tam..."

Moments later, Boomish burst into the dining room, a plate of steaming pancakes in his paw. With a flourish, he deposited them on the table in front of Blackpaw.

"Here you go Nancy," he said. "I hope you like them."

"Oh, Boomish!" Blackpaw gushed. "You're simply amazing. How did you ever—" She froze as the buttery aroma hit her nose. She leaned forward and took a sniff. Instantly her mouth began to water. "Oh, they smell heavenly," she said. "Oh thank you, Boomish. Thank you ever so much!" Unable to wait a second more, Blackpaw took a bite. Her eyes widened. "Mmoh my," she mumbled.

Back in the alleyway, Jeremiah was just slipping through the back door of the kitchen. Once inside, he tiptoed over to the counter, climbed on top, and picked up the pan Boomish had left there. Looking around, he spied another pan hanging on the wall. He pulled it down and put it next to the magic pan. The pans looked identical. "That ought to do it," he said with a nod.

Setting the ordinary pan on the counter, Jeremiah hopped down, tucked Boomish's pan under his arm, and slipped out the back door.

Boomish stared dreamily across the table at Blackpaw, who was shoveling pancakes down her maw at lightning speed. She stuffed the last bite into her overflowing mouth and stared at the empty plate, her forehead crinkled in disappointment. Then a sudden movement at the window caught her eye. It was Jeremiah's paw, his thumb sticking up.

Blackpaw gulped down her mouthful of food and said, "Well...I guess I should be going. But I can't remember when I've had such a delicious treat. And I owe it all to you, Boomish of Briarberry!"

"Oh, well, I..." Boomish muttered. Gracefully, Blackpaw put on her hat, rose from the table, and held out a paw. Boomish clutched it. "Oh, um, if you haven't had your fill of pancakes," he said, "I'll be hosting a magnificous pancake breakfast here tomorrow."

"Tomorrow?"

"Yes," he said. "Tomorrow morning at eight o'clock. And it would be delectable if you could come."

"Really?" Blackpaw said shyly. "Why, yes Boomish. I think that would be lovely. Well, until tomorrow."

"Until tomorrow," Boomish said, lost in her blue eyes. After pulling several times, Blackpaw finally wrenched her paw free from Boomish's grasp. Then she floated toward the exit, stopping every few steps to turn and wave at Boomish. He eagerly waved back. Finally, she was gone, and Boomish slumped down into the booth.

"Crivvens," he sighed.

Pancake Surprise

Boomish awoke the next morning in Judge Oddkins's room, a huge grin on his face as he recalled his enchanted evening with Nancy Skipchurch. Leaping out of bed, he pranced to the window, threw open the shutters, and flung out his arms. "What a day!" he called to the world. "What a beautiful, stupendalous day!"

On the street below, an old nanny goat in spectacles and a flowered hat squinted up at him. "Be quiet up there!" she croaked, shaking her cane.

Boomish laughed it off and glided over to the mirror. "Well, Boomish," he said to his reflection, "it looks like you're in love, my friend." He licked a paw and smoothed his eyebrows. "And what's more, she is obviously head over heels in love with you." He straightened his whiskers. "But if Nancy thinks she's in love now," he added, "wait till she sees you astound the whole town and make a little girl's birthday wish come true. She's not going to know what hit her."

He took one final look at his reflection and, seeing that he was the handsomest cat in town, picked up the bag and swung open the door. "In fact," he continued as he floated down the stairs, "she'll probably be so in love, she'll ask me to marry her, and I'll say, 'Whoa! Slow down, Nancy.'"

When Boomish reached the lobby, a buzz of noise coming from the street made him glance outside. A line of what looked to be half the town filled the narrow road. "You'd better get used to this my friend," he said to himself. "You're a celebrity now."

Giving his bag a confident pat, he strolled into the dining room. Mildred and Mollie were already there, scrambling to set the tables. "Good mornin', luv!" Mollie waved cheerfully.

Mildred looked up and barked, "Put this on and help us with the tables. After all, this is all your grand idea. T'isn't it?" She threw an apron at him. It landed on his head. Boomish opened his mouth to let the pig know that Chefs du Jour who were also beloved celebrities didn't perform such lowly tasks as setting tables, but changed his mind when Mildred glared at him as though she'd like to clamp her hooves around his fuzzy neck. He put on the apron while Mildred went back to work, muttering irritably.

Boomish grabbed a pawful of napkins and headed to a table by the window. He dropped them down, then looked outside for Nancy. The crowd had swelled to twice its previous size, and the line had dissolved into a swarm of whining, shuffling animals. The giggling girls saw him and squealed. Geraldine waved. Boomish was waving back when Mildred stomped by. "Ah, you didn't happen to see..." he began. Mildred glared. "Never mind," he said.

He pulled out a piece of paper and wrote, "Reserved for Nancy Skipchurch," on it, drawing a heart in place of the dot on the *i*. Lovingly, he set it on the table.

Mollie trotted over with some plates and cast a worried glance out the window. "Blimey!" she said. "Looks like the 'ole town has 'eard about your big breakfast." She set them down and said, "Well, we'd best let them in, eh?"

As Boomish rushed to the kitchen, Mollie opened the door and the hungry townsfolk poured in.

Through the kitchen door Boomish could hear the excited chatter of the crowd, and his heart beat faster. Quickly, he put on his hat and apron. Then he trotted to the swinging door and took a quick peek at Nancy's table. The dining room was full to bursting with a line of animals waiting to get in, but Nancy's seat was empty. "I guess Nancy's running late," Boomish said. "Isn't that just like a girl?" He smiled and shook his head. Then he pulled out the pan and used it to limber up, stretching this way and that.

In the dining room, the townsfolk began some light-hearted singing: "We want some pancakes, that much is true. You pass 'em on to me, and I'll pass 'em on to you. Hey!"

As they launched into another round, Mollie poked her head into the kitchen. "Excuse me luv, but they're ready for pancakes, if you don't mind."

"But, I was waiting for...oh, never mind. I'm sure she'll be here any minute. All right," he said. "Coming right up." Mollie nodded in relief and disappeared into the dining room.

Boomish held out the pan. "This is it," he said. "It's show time!" He took a deep breath and began the incantation. "Crick-a-pin, toss-o-tam, here upon my magic pan. Flip-o-fluff, enchant-ee-bakes, time to munch on pan-ee-cakes." Nothing happened.

"Uh..." Boomish scratched his head. "Hmm," he mumbled. "Maybe it just needs a little warming up." He shook it. He rubbed it on his rump. He tried again. "Crick-a-pin, toss-o-tam, here upon my magic pan. Flip-o-fluff, enchant-ee-bakes, time to munch on pan-ee-cakes." The pan lay like a lump of coal in Boomish's now sweaty paw.

In the dining room, the singing had turned to enthusiastic chanting. "We want pancakes! We want pancakes! We want pancakes!"

Boomish took another peek into the dining room. Some of the animals had started drooling. Mildred and Mollie ran from table to table, refilling glasses of milk, trying to keep the animals' empty tummies from rumbling too loudly.

Boomish shut the door. "Maybe it just couldn't hear me," he said hopefully. "CRICK-A-PIN, TOSS-O-TAM," he enunciated as if the pan were a deaf dog who'd misplaced his ear trumpet. Nothing. Boomish gaped at the pan. "What's wrong with this thing?" he said, his voice cracking.

Now the excited chanting sounded like a warning. "PANCAKES! PANCAKES! PANCAKES!"

Boomish jumped as Mollie stuck her head back in and said with a pained smile, "Sorry to intrude! But would you 'appen to know when we'll be seein' them pancakes?"

"Just a sec!" he squeaked. As soon as her head disappeared, Boomish desperately banged the pan on the countertop.

"I..."

Bang!

"command..."

Bang!

"you..."

Bang!

"to make..."

Bang!

"pancakes!"

BangBangBangBang!

A small foot tapped on the floor next to Boomish, and he froze. Slowly, he looked from the foot to the crossed arms and into the livid face of Desdemona. "Master Boomish, what is going on?" she demanded. "Why haven't you started the pan?"

Boomish threw himself upon the mouse crying, "Desdemona, you have to help me! The pan isn't working!"

Shooting him a look of annoyance, she grabbed the pan and recited the incantation. Nothing. "For the love of licorice, we're in a real pickle now!" she said, shoving the pan at Boomish and pacing the floor. "I had decided I'd have nothing to do with your half-baked breakfast, but when I heard all the commotion coming from the dining room, I thought I'd better see what was going on."

Boomish picked up the pan again and shook it violently. "I don't get it," he wailed. "It was working just fine last night!"

The chanting of the ravenous townsfolk had become mixed with angry growls and yeowls along with the pounding of silverware on the table. "Crikey! Would everyone please calm down?" Mollie's panicked voice came through the door.

Desdemona wrung her paws as she paced. "And now Judge Oddkins is missing. I can't find him anywhere and— Oh, Betsy! What should I do?" All at once, she stopped pacing and faced Boomish. "Master Boomish," she said, "there is nothing for it. We must face the music." She started for the door as Boomish danced nervously, the pan still clutched in his paw. When she reached the door, she squared her shoulders and pulled it open.

Screech! THUD! Thump thump thump thump! A stampede of ravenous animals was climbing over tables and knocking down chairs in a mad rush to get to the kitchen.

Desdemona slammed the door, a look of terror on her face. Whipping around, she locked eyes with Boomish. "RUN!" she screeched. Boomish's chef's hat flew off as Desdemona yanked his paw and bolted out the back door. Frantically, they ran down the alleyway, made a sharp turn down a narrow lane, and skidded onto the main street of town. All the shops were closed, and the streets were deserted.

"Crivvens," Boomish said breathlessly as he ran. "It's like a ghost town. Where is everybody?"

"Where do you think?" Desdemona wheezed, clutching her babushka to her head. "They've all gone to the Merry

Spinster for pancakes. But they're not getting any, are they!" Boomish kept his mouth shut.

As they sped around a corner and sprinted down a bumpy lane leading to the harbor, angry shouts rang out from behind them. "Oh, no!" said Desdemona. "They're on to us!"

They redoubled their efforts and ran even faster, but by the time their paws hit the splintery wood of the docks, the shouting had grown louder. Boomish glanced behind them and gulped. Thundering down the hill, raising a billowing cloud of dust, was a huge mob of angry villagers waving forks, knives, and plates and foaming at their mouths. "Eeek!" he shrieked. "They're going to kill us!"

"Not if we reach the end of this pier before they do," gasped Desdemona, jumping over a rotten board. Boomish opened his mouth to respond when a loud whistle cut through the noise of the crowd. *Tweeooweeph!* Standing on the stern of his ship, grinning at them through a telescope was Wizzencoots. He waved.

"Thank Betsy," cried Desdemona. "Hurry, Master Boomish! To the *Grizzella*, quick as you can!"

Dan was on the dock, rapidly untying the last rope from its mooring. Wizzencoots dropped the telescope and hustled over to the wheel as the ship started drifting away from the pier. "Hurry!" called Dan, waving them in. His brow crinkled in concern as he looked over at the gangplank. As the ship pulled away, it was dragging the board along with it.

"Death to Boomish of Briarberry!" someone shouted. Boomish winced, then gasped as he saw Dan grasp the end of the gangplank, fighting to keep it in place. Finally, Dan gave up and the board dropped into the water with a splash. The *Grizzella* was now two Boomish lengths away from the pier and drifting farther every second.

Boomish and Desdemona exchanged panicked looks. They'd have to jump. With Dan waving them on, his arm like a windmill, they raced the last few feet to the end of the pier and each took a flying leap over the water. Boomish sailed through the air then hit the deck with a *thud*. A second later, Desdemona landed beside him, and moments after her came Dan, who only jumped once he was sure Boomish and Desdemona had made it to safety.

Wide-eyed, Boomish ran to the railing and looked over. The front of the horde skidded to a stop as they ran out of pier. But just like a bowling ball, the ones in back smacked into them, sending those in front flying like pins into the sea.

As the animals in the water sputtered in anger, the townsfolk left on the pier hurled insults, plates, and utensils at the retreating *Grizzella*. Boomish ducked as a plate whizzed over his head. Then he stood up and watched in relief as the last of the silverware plunked harmlessly into the murky waters of the harbor.

Apology Ashmology

"**O**uch!" Boomish stood rubbing his muzzle as Desdemona dropped the whisker she'd just plucked from his face and glared at him as though she wished she could cause a lot more pain than that.

Then Dan, who'd been keeping an eye on the villagers until the ship was a safe distance away, turned to give Boomish a piece of his mind. "Well, well, well," he said. "Look who's here. Captain Pancakes, I presume? Nice apron," he added. Wincing, Boomish took it off. "You've caused an awful lot of trouble around here this morning, you know," Dan said.

Boomish cleared his throat uncomfortably. "Yes, but I didn't mean—"

"Half the town wants to tie you in a sack and throw you in the river," the big dog said.

"And the other half wants to forgive me?" Boomish asked.

"The other half wants to hang you!"

Boomish gulped. He looked over at Desdemona, but she'd turned her back on him and was on her way to the helm. Carrying the pan, Boomish moped after her.

Wizzencoots saw them coming and chuckled, "The only thing warse than an angry mob is a hoongry, angry mob, eh, Desdemona?"

"I wish I could see the humor in all of this, Wizzencoots," she answered. "But we're in quite a desperate situation at the moment. And the worst of it is that we've lost Judge Oddkins!" At the mention of the badger, Boomish jumped. He'd forgotten all about the judge.

"Well noo," Wizzencoots said, "I may be of some help in that department."

He motioned to Dan, and the big dog took over the wheel while Boomish and Desdemona followed Wizzencoots down some dingy stairs and through a narrow passage to a small room with bunk beds stacked against the walls. One of them had a curtain hanging across it. Wizzencoots shuffled over to the curtain and pulled it back. Desdemona gasped.

Lying unconscious, his head wrapped in a bandage and one arm in a sling, was Judge Oddkins. His spectacles were missing, and one eye was swollen shut. Desdemona held a paw to her mouth, a stricken look on her face. Boomish stood behind her, his lower lip trembling. "Wizzencoots, what happened?" Desdemona asked, her eyes brimming with tears.

"Well, I dinnae mind tellin' yeu there was a bit o' mischief goin' on here last night," Wizzencoots began. "Danny and I were up on deck doin' a bit o' last minute prep work an' some sock mending. I've always got time teu give some attention teu me beauties," he said, showing them off with some fancy dance steps. Impatiently, Desdemona cleared her throat. Wizzencoots frowned, but went on with his story. "Och, where was I? Right. Danny an me hear a commotion comin' from down the dock. We take a look-see an' spy some figures wrastlin' in the dark."

"Could you tell who they were?" Desdemona asked.

"Cannae say precisely," said Wizzencoots with a shake of his head. "I can tell yeu, they were teu o' the strangest scoundrels I've ever taken a gander at. As near as I could tell, the short one was a farmer and the tall one was in a ball gown." He shrugged then continued, "An' yeu know how two against one gets me dander up!" Wizzencoots shook a paw at the injustice. "So Danny boy an' I, we hustled our bahookies down there fast as we could. Boot as soon as they spied us comin', they ran for town, an' when I took a look see at who their victim was,"—he motioned to the sleeping badger—"well, we thought it best teu attend teu him farst."

Desdemona nodded. "You did the right thing, Wizzencoots," she said.

Boomish stood behind her looking crushed. He was responsible for the state Judge Oddkins was in. Because of his selfishness, the judge had almost lost his life.

Suddenly Judge Oddkins mumbled and waved his free arm as he came to. "Back!" he cried. "Back, I say! You've bitten off more than you can chew this time."

Desdemona leaned over to restrain the flailing arm. "Easy, judge," she said. "You're among friends now."

"Desdemona, is that you?" Judge Oddkins asked, blinking at the smallest of three blurry shapes in front of him. Shakily, he reached his paw to his nose, searching for his glasses.

"Dinnae worry about yeur spectacles, Judge," Wizzencoots said. "Danny boy will fix em up good as new in no time."

Judge Oddkins smiled gratefully. "And there's young Master Boomish," he said, a twinkle in his one open eye. "Oh," he said in dismay as he noticed the pan Boomish was carrying. "Don't tell me I missed a delicious pancake breakfast." Being reminded of his food fiasco was too much for Boomish. He burst into tears. "Now, now, what's all this, my boy?" Judge Oddkins inquired over Boomish's loud sobs.

"I..." Boomish began, his voice trembling. "I—it's all my fault." He turned to Desdemona, his eyes pleading for understanding. "It's—it's my fault that Judge Oddkins was on the dock last night," he wheezed, wringing his paws. "I didn't want to work on the *Grizzella*, so I told Judge Oddkins they gave his room away and he—he went to go sleep on the ship and I—and I—" He choked on a sob. "And now the whole town hates me!" Boomish burst into tears.

"Master Boomish!" exclaimed Desdemona, not believing her ears.

But Judge Oddkins raised a paw. "Now, now, Desdemona. I'm all right," he said. "And the important thing is that nothing has happened to Master Boomish here."

Desdemona begged to differ, but seeing the weary look on Judge Oddkins's face she said, "Now, Judge, we've got some talking to do. And you must rest." The badger smiled and drifted off to sleep as Desdemona pulled the curtain back in place.

Then Desdemona and Boomish, who wiped his nose with a paw, followed Wizzencoots farther down the passageway to the galley. When they squeezed inside the small room, Wizzencoots made a sweeping motion with his paw and said proudly, "This is where the magic happens!" Bolted to the middle of the floor was a rectangular table with a few chairs pushed up to it. Along the side walls were shelves stuffed with cans of Cap'n Vom Vom's cream of mushroom soup, bags of dried beans, and other pantry staples. In the back of the room was a small stove, and an assortment of pots, pans, and cooking utensils.

Exhausted, Desdemona collapsed into a chair. Boomish sniffled, set the pan on the table, and sat down across from her. Wizzencoots stood scratching his chin. "So where teu now, señorita?" he asked the mouse. "I'm nae expert, but I think the judge is going teu need some medical attention."

"I agree, Wizzencoots," replied Desdemona. "But before we decide where to take him, there's something I need to examine." She leveled her eyes at him. "For some reason, the pan isn't working."

"Nae workin'?" Wizzencoots scowled. "Here, let me take a gander if yeu dinnae mind." Boomish slid the pan across the table, and Wizzencoots began a thorough examination. He started with a long sniff, then tapped it, listening intently.

Meanwhile, Desdemona was staring intently into Boomish's teary eyes. "What?" he said.

"What was that you said back at the Merry Spinster, about the pan working just fine last night?" she began.

"Oh, that," Boomish said, perking up at the reminder of the lovely Nancy. "Well, you see," he said, wiping his eyes, "there was this girl and, well, she was hungry." He paused, taking note of Desdemona's disapproving frown. "And the kitchen was closed, and well, she was practically starving, and, well,"—he threw his paws up in exasperation—"what's the point of having a magic pan if you never get to use it?"

"Hoohoo! Oh my, oh my!" Wizzencoots whiskey laughed, slapping his knee. "Was yeur head tarned by a pretty face?" Boomish turned a dark shade of pink, and Wizzencoots got back to his examination, chuckling as he *tinked* and *tonked* the pan.

"So you used the pan?" said Desdemona.

"Yes," Boomish said softly.

"And was it ever out of your sight?"

Boomish scrunched his eyebrows together, thinking hard as Desdemona's eyes burned into him. "Um..." he began.

"Well noo, here's yeur problem," Wizzencoots said. "Yeu've got the wrong pan!" He flipped it over and held it out. Etched into the black metal bottom of the pan were the words "Property of the Merry Spinster."

"Master Boomish!" Desdemona shrieked. "How could you have let this happen?"

"But—wha—how—" Boomish garbled.

"Don't you see?" she said. "This girl, this—"

"Nancy," he mumbled.

"This Nancy switched pans on you!"

Boomish opened his mouth to defend the fair maiden, but Wizzencoots boomed, "An now she's got the magic pan, an yeu've got egg on yeur face!"

Boomish's day had gone from blissful to not so hot, to bad, then really, really bad, and now it seemed it couldn't get any worse. Trying to control the tears threatening to leak from his eyes, he looked at Desdemona and quavered, "OK, so...so I know, losing the pan...not so good. But is the pan really *that* important? Can't we just get another one at the Lemon Meringues?"

Desdemona leapt to her feet and stared at Boomish in amazement. "No!" she shrieked. "The pan is irreplaceable! One of a kind! Even if we discount the small matter of the islands' being practically defenseless without it, if you don't have the pan and the Master Book of Recipes in your possession when you take the Oath of Desserts, the magic won't work, and you'll never become the Master Sweet Smith!"

"Oh," Boomish whispered hoarsely.

"Oh, Betsy," she sighed, looking to the heavens. "The pan must've made a mistake. The real Master Smith would never be so foolish!" Boomish looked down at the table, mortified.

Wizzencoots cleared his throat uncomfortably and said, "So teu find the pan, it stands teu reason yeu have teu find this Nancy character." Desdemona nodded, pacing the floor. "Well noo, that could take a bit o' time," he mused. "She's likely teu be anywhere."

"I agree," Desdemona said. She stopped pacing and fixed her eyes on Wizzencoots. "And since the timer is ticking, there's only one thing to do." Boomish sniffled and looked up. Wizzencoots leaned closer. "We've got to see *the owl.*"

The dog's eyes bulged, and he began coughing uncontrollably. "Desdemona," he wheezed, "I hope yeu dinnae say what I thought yeu did." When she didn't answer, he hopped around the room, waving his arms and sputtering, "Trickery! Treachery! Double-dealing!" Boomish wiped the tears from his eyes and stared as Wizzencoots continued his tirade. "Yeu know I'd never have agreed to take yeu if I knew yeu were goin' teu see that hootin' huckster!"

"I know full well your feelings about witchcraft," Desdemona said. "And it's certainly no secret Nitty Pitty Ulu has earned her infamous reputation."

"Exactly my point," Wizzencoots grumbled.

"And," the mouse said, "had I realized we'd be in need of her services, I never would've asked you for help."

The old dog glared at the mouse, his paws on his hips. "I would've thought yeu'd have better sense than that."

"Absolutely," she said. "So feel free to drop Master Boomish and me off at the nearest port, and we'll find other transportation."

"Done!" he barked, his arms crossed. Boomish looked from Wizzencoots to Desdemona in dismay.

"Although," Desdemona said, "I must admit I'm a bit surprised." Wizzencoots cocked an ear as Desdemona continued, "I didn't think *you* of all dogs would let a silly, old bird get in the way of helping an old friend."

Boomish held his breath as the creases in Wizzencoots's forehead grew deeper and deeper. "Och! Grousin' mulligrubs!" the dog spat. "Fine. Just dinnae expect me teu say teu words to that feathered phony!" Desdemona held out her paws in mock surrender, and Boomish exhaled in relief. "Well, enough o' this jabber nowling," growled the old dog. "We've got work teu do." He leaned over the table and stared deeply into Boomish's and Desdemona's eyes. "Gentlemen—" he said in his gravelly voice.

"Ahem," coughed Desdemona.

"...and lady," Wizzencoots added, "prepare yourselves. This is no longer a pleasure cruise. It's a rescue operation!"

Once Wizzencoots agreed to sail to the Creephanger Crags, home of Nitty Pitty Ulu, he and Desdemona checked the charts for a suitable spot to drop Judge Oddkins. After much debate, they decided upon St. Gustafson's Home for Wayward Sailors. A prison wasn't an ideal place to leave the judge, but not only was it en route, it also had an infirmary where the judge could be tended to until Wizzencoots returned to take him back to Briarberry.

While the other two were talking, Boomish sat in thought. He'd opened his big mouth and promised the town a pancake breakfast. He'd lost the pan. He'd been tricked by Nancy. And then there was Geraldine. And the *Pudding*. And what about Judge Oddkins? "Crivvens," Boomish whispered, tears welling up in his eyes as the weight of all of his mistakes came crashing down on him. "He could've died!"

Wizzencoots and Desdemona stopped talking and looked across the table at him. Fighting back the tears, Boomish took a breath and said shakily, "I—I know I've made a lot of mistakes." Wizzencoots rolled his eyes and started to speak, but Desdemona cut him off, holding up her paw. "But if

I'm—*sniff*—going to be the Master Dessert King or whatever it's called," Boomish continued, "then I've got to start acting like it. So I promise that from now on, I'm going to be responderous and try to make up for everything I've done."

Desdemona locked eyes with Boomish. "Master Boomish," she said, "I'm glad you've finally realized what a great disappointment you've been. Time after time," she said, her voice becoming squeakier and squeakier, "you've put yourself first; before your friends, before your duties, even before the fate of the Lemon Meringue Islands!" Boomish's ears drooped. Wizzencoots studied a grease spot on the ceiling. "And as for making up for your mistakes," Desdemona said with a sad shake of her head, "well, I just don't see how you can." Without another word, she got up and marched out of the galley.

"Well noo," Wizzencoots said as he rose from his seat. "I guess I'd, I'd best be—it's time teu—och!" he said and shuffled after her.

With a heart as heavy as the *Grizzella's* anchor, Boomish pushed back his chair and wandered out of the galley. A few minutes later he found himself standing in front of Judge Oddkins's bunk. Quietly, he pulled back the curtain and looked down upon the sleeping badger. "Judge Oddkins?" he whispered.

With a small snort, the judge opened his eyes. "Master Boomish. How are you, my boy?"

"Oh, Judge, I'm so, so sorry!" said Boomish, as the tears he'd been holding in ran down cheeks. "I'm really, really—*hic*—sorry about what happened to you, for losing the pan, for everything! *Bahaa*!"

"There, there, my boy," Judge Oddkins said while Boomish had a good cry.

When he was done, the young cat reached for the curtain and blew his nose while Judge Oddkins pretended not to notice. Then Boomish wiped his eyes said, "Back at the orphanage when I *maybe* made a mistake or two, they weren't *that* big of a deal. I mean nobody got hurt or anything. But since I've left the orphanage, they've all been a big deal, and I've hurt everybody!"

"My, my," said the judge. "I see how that's upsetting."

"Yes!" Boomish blurted out. "And I promised Desdemona I would make things right and be a real Master of Desserts, and she said..." Boomish choked back a sob and continued, "she said that she didn't see how I could. And now I think she's right! And I don't even know how to be a Master Dessert King anyway."

The badger held up his paw. "Now, now, now, my boy," he said, shaking his bandaged head. "Try to fix everything at once, and you'll give up before you even start. Just take things one step at a time, and you'll do fine. You'll see."

Boomish was quiet for a moment, his brow furrowed in thought. "So first, maybe I just try to get back the pan?"

"Yes, yes. That's right," said Judge Oddkins with a yawn. "And as for being a real Master Sweet Smith, well, all I can tell you is that throughout the history of the Lemon Meringue Islands, creatures of all kinds have been Master Smiths. There've been dogs and cats, rabbits and cows, to name a few. But although they all had their special qualities, they did share one thing in common."

"What's that?" Boomish asked with a sniff.

"They always put the needs of others before their own." As Boomish considered this, Judge Oddkins's eyelids began to droop. "You mean sometimes," Boomish corrected.

"M'boy, I mean *all* th tme," the Judge mumbled.

"Most of the time?" Boomish said.

"All...of...*uhhhuh*...the...time." And Judge Oddkins was fast asleep.

A New Leaf

After his talk with Judge Oddkins, Boomish wandered up to the main deck. As he stepped out into the sunshine, the fresh sea air blowing through his fur lifted his spirits, and he padded over to the others, determined to act like a king.

"Well, noo," Wizzencoots was saying, "by my reckoning, after we drop off the judge at St. Gustafson's, we've got another teu days at sea before we get teu the Creephanger Crags an that walking feather duster." He made a face like he'd bitten into a lemon.

"Two days?" said Desdemona. "Even if we sail around the clock?"

"Well since there are only three of us who can man the wheel at night, there just aren't enough of us to do it," Dan said.

"Actually, Dan, there are four of us," Boomish said as he finished counting. "So we do have enough crew to sail at night. Right?" He waited while Wizzencoots coughed uncomfortably, and Dan avoided his stare. "What?" Boomish asked, looking around the circle.

"Master Boomish," said Desdemona, "after what happened to the *Pudding*, I've decided that you should keep to other parts of the ship."

Boomish was crestfallen. But remembering his vow to change, he straightened his shoulders and said, "Desdemona, I know I was irresponderous and crashed the other ship. But if you please just give me one more chance, I promise I won't crash this one."

Desdemona glanced quizzically at Wizzencoots and Dan while Boomish did his best to look responsible, which only made him look confused. Still refusing to meet Boomish's eyes, Dan shook his head no. Boomish's heart sank. Wizzencoots, however, enjoyed living dangerously. He scratched his chin then shrugged, and Boomish stood a bit taller.

After a long pause, Desdemona spoke. "I can't believe I'm taking such a chance, but I just don't see any other way to make up for all of our lost time."

Boomish clapped his paws in excitement, then quickly put on his responsible face again. "I won't disappoint you, Desdemona," he said. "I promise."

"Well, noo that that's settled, we can assign the ship's duties," Wizzencoots said, unrolling a sheet of parchment and squinting at it.

Boomish leaned in, his ears perked for the words "Captain Boomish."

"Let's see..." Wizzencoots muttered. "Desdemona, yeu'll be the navigator."

"Certainly," she replied.

"Danny, I think it just makes sense teu have yeu do all the heavy liftin'—sails an rigging an such."

"Aye, aye, Gramps," said Dan.

"An that brings me teu yeu, young Boomish," Wizzencoots said. "Tell me, just where do yeu see yeurself fittin' in?"

"How about captain?" Boomish suggested.

Wizzencoots ignored the question and asked, "Tell me, how did yeu pass yeur days at Dismal Manor?"

"Oh!" Boomish puffed out his chest. "Well, I protestated about stuff, put on plays, cooked up some yummies when I could, was team captain for *everything*." He paused. His chest had tightened at the mention of the orphanage. "I sure do miss Jack," he whispered.

"How's that?" Wizzencoots said.

"I mean, I don't know what they're doing without me, actually," he said tremulously.

At the mention of cooking, Dan's ears perked up. "Did you hear that, Gramps?" he said, his tail wagging hopefully. "Boomish knows how to cook."

The old dog shot him a warning look. "There's only one chef aboard this ship an' he's standin' right here," he said, jabbing a paw into his own chest. Dan's tail stopped wagging. "Anythin' else?" Wizzencoots asked Boomish.

"Well...I did have to scrub a pot or two, sometimes," Boomish admitted.

"Brilliant!" cried Wizzencoots. "Just what I was hopin' far." Boomish lit up and leaned forward in anticipation. "From now on, yeu're our official deck boy." Dan winced at Boomish's bad luck, then strode off to adjust the sails.

Boomish clapped his paws. "Deck boy," he said. "Fantabulous! Where do I start?"

"Right here," said the dog, pointing to one of dozens of tarnished brass posts screwed all over the deck. He handed Boomish a rag and said, "The cleats need a polish." Boomish's ears drooped. "An then there's the sail mendin', swabbin' the deck, barnacle duty, an the like. As far me, I'm off teu the galley teu prepare our first seafarin' feast. Tonight's special: seaweed an clam ragout!"

Wizzencoots danced off to the galley, leaving Boomish looking dejectedly at the rag. A few feet away, Desdemona pretended to examine a chart while she waited for Boomish to come up with some excuse as to why manual labor was not his cup of milk. But to her surprise, Boomish pointed his ears, squatted down, and started polishing the first cleat. For the rest of the day, the mouse kept a watchful eye on her charge as he polished away without complaint.

By sunset, Boomish's back was aching and his arm felt like rubber, but he was almost through with his last cleat. Dan, who'd finished his duties and was sitting against a mast and whittling a piece of wood, cast his expert eye over Boomish's work. "You missed a spot," he said.

Boomish opened his mouth to argue, but instead took a second look at the cleat. Seeing a speck of rust, he took a breath and said, "Thank you, Dan." Dan lifted an eyebrow in surprise, then nodding approvingly, went back to his carving.

As Boomish shined up the spot, an odor of old socks mixed with rotting fish hit his nostrils. Smacking a paw over his nose, he looked over at Dan and said, "Whad is thad orrible sbell?"

Before Dan could answer, Wizzencoots poked his head out of the stairwell, rang a triangle, and cried, "Dinner is sarved!"

"There's your answer," said Dan, getting up and padding toward the stairs. "I hope you're not too hungry," he added, his voice echoing in the narrow passage.

"What do you mean?" Boomish asked, as he followed Dan. "I'm star—" He stopped mid-word as he entered the galley and was almost knocked over by the stench. "Dere id is agaid!" he gasped, breathing through his mouth.

He stepped up to the stove where Wizzencoots proudly shoved a bowl of slimy brown liquid at him, and suddenly Boomish realized with horror what he was smelling was dinner. Holding the bowl as far from his nose as possible, Boomish sat down.

Wizzencoots fixed himself an extra large helping, took a seat next to Desdemona, grabbed a spoon, and said, "Well noo, dinnae be shy. Dig in everyone!" For the next few minutes, the only sounds were the loud slurping of Wizzencoots's enthusiastic eating and the occasional gagging of the other diners as they tried to swallow their first bites of seaweed and clam ragout.

Once Wizzencoots was done, he belched loudly and pushed back his chair. "Ahh," he said, patting his rounded tummy. "There's nae like dinner at sea. Well, I'd best be off teu the helm. I see the rest o' yeu are still savorin' yeur supper. Take yeur time. There's nae rush." Then he plodded out the door.

As soon as he was gone, Boomish pushed back his bowl. "This is disgustamous," he complained. "How are we supposed to eat this?"

"We don't," said Dan. Picking up his bowl, he walked over to the porthole and dumped the stinky slop into the ocean. Then he opened a cupboard and pulled out three rock-hard biscuits. He tossed one to Boomish, handed another to Desdemona, and popped the last one into his mouth, cringing as he bit down.

"Well," Desdemona said, "we'd best get back to work." She and Dan headed for the passageway, but Boomish had other ideas.

After twenty minutes had gone by with no sign of Boomish, Desdemona was about to send Dan to look for him when a heavenly smell filled their nostrils. "What's that?" Dan asked her, licking his lips and sniffing the air.

"I'm not sure," said Desdemona, walking toward the stairs. "But I think we should find out."

At the helm, Wizzencoots's nose was working, too. Quickly, he tied up the wheel and followed Dan and Desdemona to the galley, where Boomish was setting four plates on the table.

"Oh, hello," he said when he saw them. "Care to join me for some seafood soufflé?" Dan and Desdemona quickly sat down and started eating. But Wizzencoots stood in the doorway, a suspicious scowl on his face.

"That's nae proper seafarin' food. I wouldnae touch it if I were yeu!" he warned Dan and Desdemona as they ate, *mmming* and *ohhing* over Boomish's delicious meal. Finally, Wizzencoots's stomach got the better of him. He sat down and took a bite. His eyes widened with surprise and delight, and he quickly ate another forkful, and then another. Soon his plate was empty, and he glanced hopefully around for more.

"So, Wizzencoots," Desdemona said as she licked a crumb from a whisker, "it seems as though you enjoyed Master Boomish's dinner."

"Wasnae bad," the old dog said noncommittally as he eyed Dan's soufflé.

Dan slid a protective arm around his plate and said, "Maybe we could give Boomish a shot at being the ship's cook. What'dya think, Gramps?"

Wizzencoots looked down at his empty plate. "Well noo," he said as his pride battled with his stomach. His stomach growled, and he gave in. "Alright. I suppose we could give him a go. On a trial basis," he added sternly.

"Thank you, Wizzencoots," said Boomish.

"Yes, thank you!" chimed Dan and Desdemona.

Wizzencoots waved a dismissive paw, then pushed back his chair. "See yeu on deck," he said as he exited the room.

Desdemona finished her last bite of soufflé and considered Boomish from across the table. "Master Boomish," she began, "that was..."

"Yes, Desdemona?"

"That was...thank you for dinner," she said finally.

Boomish swelled with pride. But this was a different kind of pride. Instead being better than someone else, he'd been of service to someone else. It was a good feeling. "You're welcome, Desdemona," he said.

Desdemona nodded, then looked up at Dan. "We'd best get ourselves up on deck to prepare for the night's sail," she said to him. "And Master Boomish," she added, "please hurry along. We'll need you as well." She and Dan headed out the door while Boomish began tidying up the galley.

Some time later, Desdemona looked up from her charts. "What is keeping Master Boomish?" she said with a frown. Putting down the parchment, she headed down the stairs and poked her head into the sparkling clean galley. Boomish wasn't there. Puzzled, she walked along the narrow passageway until she came to the sleeping quarters. She peeked inside and her mouth dropped open.

Sitting before Judge Oddkins's bunk with a plate of soufflé in his paw, was Boomish. As Desdemona watched, the cat took a spoonful of food and gently deposited it in the badger's mouth.

"Well, well," she said softly as she backed out of the doorway.

Desdemona was just rolling up her maps when Boomish appeared on deck. "There you are, Master Boomish," she said. "Is everything ship shape down below?"

"Yes, Desdemona," he said. "And I'm ready to help some more. What do you need me to do?"

"Well, you could find Dan," she said. "I don't know where he disappeared to." As Boomish turned to go, she added, "Oh, and Master Boomish? I suppose you've earned the first night shift."

"Really, Desdemona?" he asked, dancing with excitement.

"Yes, really," she said with a smile.

Boomish was smiling back when Dan came up from below waving a hand accordion.

"Hey, Gramps," he called as he joined the group. "Look what I found!"

Wizzencoots, who was steering the ship, eagerly eyed the instrument then looked away. "Och, I dinnae know Danny. It's been a long day."

"Whadya say, Gramps?" Dan said. "How about a song?"

Wizzencoots called over his shoulder, "I'm nae in the mood, Danny."

"Aw, come on Gramps," Dan said. "This is Boomish's first real voyage. He's got to hear at least one song." Boomish looked up at Dan gratefully. Dan smiled warmly in return and played a few lilting chords on his accordion.

Wizzencoots turned around, the gentle notes softening his mood. "Yeu know," he said, a faraway look in his squinty eyes, "bein' out at sea again makes an old dog like me think o' all the companionship he's had over the years. Such warm times." He sighed. "Alright, Danny, yeur on. What's say we do 'Me Beauties'?"

Dan hit a sour chord. "Um, are you sure Gramps?" he said, the accordion frozen in his paws. "It's just, that one tends to make you a little emotional."

"'Tis nothing wrong with a bit o' feelin'!" Wizzencoots scolded. Boomish and Dan exchanged a look while Desdemona put a paw over her mouth to hide her smile. Dan rolled his eyes but obligingly squeezed out the intro to the song.

Wizzencoots waited for his cue, closed his eyes, and sang softly, "Yeu kept me snug, yeu kept me warm, and always kept yeur supple form. The nights were long an bitter cold, yet yeur embrace was good as gold. Ever true yeu cling to me as I teu yeuuuu!" The dog's voice rose to a howl. "Me beauties, me beauties, I'll always be grateful, me beauties. An though I try, I can't deny, some of their names have slipped me mind. Sally, Alice, ma Jenny, Suzette, those are names I'll never forget. *An so I sing this song of luv teu yeuuuu!*" He howled again, and Dan winced. "Me beauties," Wizzencoots sang hoarsely, "me beauties, I'll always luv me beauties." As the last notes from the accordion drifted off over the sea, Wizzencoots gazed lovingly down at his socks. Dan rolled his eyes, and Boomish giggled.

Desdemona smiled to herself as she checked her pocket watch. "It's time for the night watch," she said, snapping it shut. "Master Boomish, I believe I promised you the honors."

Boomish jumped to his feet, eager to get started. But Wizzencoots licked a paw and held it up in the breeze. "Och," he said, squinting up at the clear sky. "I dinnae know, Desdemona. I could be wrong, but I dinnae like the look of this weather. Maybe the wee laddie should take a tarn another night." Dan followed Wizzencoots's gaze while Desdemona sniffed the air, her whiskers quivering.

"Oh, Desdemona, please let me take the wheel tonight," Boomish begged. "Please, please, please! I can do it. I know I can."

Detecting only slightly raised levels of moisture in the air, Desdemona gave in. "All right," she said, "as long as you realize there's a slim chance of rain." Boomish clapped his paws and ran to the helm. Wizzencoots shook his head in disagreement with the mouse, but he toddled to the wheel and untied the ropes that had been holding the ship's heading somewhat steady.

"Just keep her dead on this course," he told the cat. "Comprende?" Boomish nodded, his feet dancing excitedly. As the dog turned to go, a gust of wind blew across the deck, ruffling Boomish's fur and buffeting the sails.

Wizzencoots paused. "Good luck, laddie," he said. "May the gods o' the sea throw yeu a bone tonight." He padded off after the others to get some sleep, and Boomish was alone.

Well, this is easy, thought Boomish as he held the wheel. He saluted his imaginary crew and called out, "Captain Boomish, sailing the ship and not crashing into anything." Chuckling to himself, he tapped a paw on the wheel and gazed up at the starry sky. "Yep," he said. "No problem." Another gust of wind brought his attention back to the sparkling sea, and he noticed the waves were much darker than before. Looking up, he searched for the moon, but all he could see was a wall of black clouds. The wind picked up, whistling through the rigging, and roiling whitecaps appeared on the waves. Boomish frowned as he gripped the wheel, which now seemed to have a life of its own.

As he struggled to keep the ship on course, a flash of lightning lit up the sky and—*boom!*—a clap of thunder exploded above his head. Seconds later, the clouds broke open, dumping buckets of rain onto Boomish and the *Grizzella*. "Ack!" he sputtered, water pouring into his eyes. The waves grew into huge swells that lifted the ship up and down like a piece of driftwood. Boomish wrestled with the relentlessly spinning wheel as the storm raged on. "I won't give up!" Boomish called into the screaming wind.

The night dragged on, and Boomish's eyelids drooped. Then his head dropped to his chest. He yanked it up again and pulled on his whiskers to stay awake.

Hours later, the wind died down. The rain stopped, and the sea calmed. In the distance, a blush of pink spread across the gray horizon and Desdemona appeared from below. As she carried her maps to the helm, she spied Boomish, soaking wet and barely awake, slumped against the wheel. She nodded proudly.

Later that day, after a heartfelt good-bye to Judge Oddkins, Boomish stood at the stern of the *Flying Grizzella*, watching as the walls of St. Gustafson's grew smaller and smaller.

Seeing Boomish alone, Desdemona wandered over, and the two of them stood together, lost in their own thoughts. After a few minutes, Boomish broke the silence. "Desdemona," he said, unable to meet her eyes, "do you still think the pan made a mistake when it picked me?"

The mouse frowned as she recalled her harsh words. "Oh my," she said. "I suppose I did say that, didn't I." Boomish nodded, and Desdemona took his paw in hers. "Master Boomish," she said, "I may have thought so at the time, but watching you these last two days has reminded me of something very important."

"What?" Boomish asked.

"That none of us are born perfectly baked." Boomish cocked his head in confusion as Desdemona continued. "No," she said. "It takes time to make a perfect cheesecake. Why, even after it's pulled from the oven, it still has a little more firming up to do." She turned and looked up into his face. "Don't you see?" she smiled. "You just needed a little time to firm up."

"So, I'm a cheesecake?" Boomish said.

"Hmm...maybe more like a pumpkin pie."

Nitty Pitty Ulu

Wizzencoots stood at the wheel of the *Flying Grizzella*, a sour look on his face as a dark and dreary coastline shrouded in mist came into view. "There they are," he muttered, "the Creephanger Crags." He called over to Desdemona, who was standing on the bow with Boomish, "I hope yeu're happy!" Desdemona ignored him.

Dan tossed the anchor into the icy, gray water and then began to untie the jolly boat from where it hung on the side of the ship. "Come on, everyone," he said, holding onto the rope. They all climbed in, and Dan lowered the boat into the sea. It landed with a *splunk*. Desdemona hopped onto the bow while Wizzencoots tucked his legs under him, trying to protect his beauties from the salty sea spray. Dan picked up the oars, and Boomish watched in awe as the big dog rowed the small boat through the choppy sea like it was a sled on a frozen lake.

Much too soon for Wizzencoots, they were stepping onto the black pebble beach of the island. "Och!" he grumbled, scowling at the seaweed-covered rocks scattered across the shore. "Isna this perfect? A miserable home far a miserable charlatan!"

Thick fog swirled around them as Desdemona led the way up the beach toward the towering black boulders that stood sentry on the shoreline. Her whiskers twitched as she poked around the rocks. "Where is it?" she said. "I know it's around here somewhere...ah! There it is." Spying a narrow opening between two boulders, she squeezed through and emerged onto a trail leading up a stony hillside. As the other animals followed her through the mist, the only sounds were the crunch of paws on the pebbly path and Wizzencoots's disgruntled muttering.

Boomish's stomach fluttered nervously as he said to himself, "Who is this Nitty Pitty Ulu anyway? And why does Wizzencoots hate her so much? And what if she can't tell us where the pan is? What if she can't tell us anything?" By the time they reached the end of the trail, Boomish was so distracted he walked right into Dan's backside. "Oops!" he said.

Shooting straight up in front of them was a smooth, sheer, gray rock face. Boomish tilted back his head, looking for the top, but it was lost in the mist. At the base of the towering boulder was a wooden platform, half the size of the ship's galley, with sides constructed of pieces of driftwood nailed together by someone who was obviously not a carpenter. Hanging down into the box was a series of ropes and pulleys, creating a crude elevator.

Desdemona stepped onto the lift, and Dan and Boomish followed suit, but Wizzencoots stopped short. "I'll nae take one step onto that contraption," he insisted, looking at the homemade elevator fearfully. "It's a deathtrap!"

"Aw, come on, Gramps," Dan urged. "It's fine." He tugged on a pulley to show Wizzencoots it was in working condition.

Desdemona tapped her foot impatiently. "Wizzencoots," she said, "I have no time for theatrics. You know perfectly well the lift is safe, and you will join us immediately."

Reluctantly, the old dog clambered aboard. Slowly, Dan began pulling them up. *Eek! Eek! Eek!* went the rusty wheels, each tug bringing them a little farther up the side of the cliff. The damp air grew colder, and Boomish shivered. After what seemed like ages, a dark hole appeared above them, and as they got closer, it revealed itself as the entrance to a cave. Once the platform reached the mouth of the cave, the lift jerked to a stop. Dan tied the rope to a claw-shaped handle sticking out of the mountainside, and one by one, the animals stepped into the dim chamber.

An icy draft sent giant feathers swirling in miniature tornadoes across the limestone floor. Purple stalactites hung like giant fangs from the ceiling, their shadows dancing over the cave walls. In the middle of the room, a large iron cauldron sat over a blue-green fire, and hunched behind the pot with her back to them was an enormous owl. Her dusty brown and black feathers stuck out at crazy angles. Strands of seaweed hung from her door-sized wings, and two feathery ear tufts shot out like fountains from the top of her square head. Slowly, the owl began to chant:

And from the waves the travelers come,
Cold and wet and somewhat glum,
They're seeking not my company,
But a favor most dire to ask of me.

"Hazza!" she screeched as she whirled around, seaweed flying from her outstretched wings. The flames under the pot flared up toward the ceiling, and a cloud of thick, orange smoke exploded from the cauldron. Wizzencoots cursed, Boomish yelped, and Dan winced. Desdemona waited, her arms crossed.

Slowly, the huge bird tucked her wings back to her sides, cocked her head, and eyed the interlopers through a pair of shiny gold spectacles resting on the bridge of her beak. "Welcome, Desdemona, Dan, and...Boomish!" she said in a deep, booming voice that echoed through cave. Boomish and Dan's mouths dropped open in amazement.

"Hello, Nitty Pitty," Desdemona said.

"And that tail I see must belong to the superstitious Wizzencoots," said the owl, her voice now high and scratchy.

Wizzencoots, who'd been trying to avoid detection, stepped out from behind Dan and said, "Aye, that'd be me. Boot dinnae think for a minute that I'm impressed with yeur wee parlor trick, 'cause I'm not." He eyed the owl, doing his best to look unimpressed. "I've seen better card tricks at the Merry Spinster."

The great owl lifted an eyebrow, and Wizzencoots sidled closer to Dan. "I," she said, ruffling her feathers and widening her eyes, "am the Great Nitty Pitty Ulu!" She marched slowly back and forth, her sharp talons scratching the floor with each step. "Welcome to my home."

"Yes, we all know who you are, Nitty Pitty," said Desdemona. "Now the reason we're here—"

"Just a minute," Nitty Pitty interrupted. "I like to know a little something about my clients before I start working, if you don't mind." Circling a wingtip, she zeroed in on Boomish and said, "Why don't we start with...you?"

Boomish jumped. "Who me? Well, um, I'm from Briarberry and—"

"Oh! Is that where you're from?" exclaimed the owl, hopping from one foot to the other.

"You know perfectly well where he's from, Nitty Pitty," Desdemona said.

Nitty Pitty shot her a look and said to Boomish, "Please, continue. This is most interesting. So, you left Briarberry. Then where did you go?"

Boomish opened his mouth to answer but Desdemona cut in, "Nitty Pitty, we're in rather a hurry, so if you don't mind could you please get down to—"

"Tut tut!" Nitty Pitty clacked her beak, glaring at the mouse through her spectacles. "I'll be asking the questions, Desdemona, not you." Desdemona rolled her eyes as the owl stomped over to the cauldron. "And speaking of questions"—she reached behind it and pulled out an iron frying pan—"Hungry anyone?" Holding her wings around her belly the owl hooted with laughter. Boomish turned beet red. Dan winced in sympathy.

"All right, Nitty Pitty," Desdemona scolded. "You've had your fun. Now can you please tell us where the pan is?"

"Hoo *hoo*! Hoo *hoo*!" the owl laughed, holding up a wingtip while she tried to compose herself. Finally, she said, "If you insist, but first things first. We haven't agreed on the particulars."

"Particulars?" Boomish whispered to Dan.

"Her payment," Dan answered quietly.

"Once I get back to the Lemon Meringues, I'll have your usual order delivered immediately," said Desdemona, tapping her foot.

"Not so fast," said the owl, swiveling her head around so her beak was less than an inch from Desdemona's nose.

"Rumor has it that the Lemon Meringues have been having some trouble with supply and distribution lately. So who knows *when* I'd get my chocolate fluffles. No," she said, continuing her circuit, "I think I'm going to require something else."

Desdemona raised an eyebrow while Wizzencoots called out from his position beside Dan, "I'd like teu hear a wee bit more about this somethin' else yeu're hootin' about."

"Certainly," said the owl. Spreading her great wings, she spoke in a deep and ominous tone. "First, you must travel to the Sorrowful Shores of Malfinor, where you must choose, from among you, a champion."

"A champion?" said Dan. "What for?"

"To do battle," boomed the owl.

"Battle?" asked Boomish.

"Yes, battle!" hissed the owl, her eyes bulging. "One of you must defeat, uhh, must defeat Alfinor, the mighty and dreadful, one-armed clam digger."

"Alfinor from Malfinor?" Desdemona said.

"That's right," Nitty Pitty said, then continued. "If, by some miracle, your champion survives, the clam digger will then be obliged to divulge the secret location of the long lost map of, um, Old King Clangdimum. This map, if the stories are true, should lead you through the, uhhh, through the Haunted Valley of Ding Dangdimum. And, if by some miraculous turn of events, you should survive that, then the path should take you to the cave of Lord Fouldamore the Smelly, where, if you're lucky, you—"

"So, wait a minute. You want us to bring you the map?" asked Dan, scratching his head.

"No, no!" Nitty Pitty cackled. "The map is important to be sure, but it is only one of the enchanted items you'll need if your quest is to be successful."

"Well, what else do we need?" said Boomish.

"Oh," Nitty Pitty scratched her head with a wing. "Let me see now, um, well, uh, oh yes! The other enchanted items shall include, but are not limited to the, um, the twelve golden marbles of Saint Garbles, um, all six heads of the dreaded fish monger of, uh, Flounder! Yes, Flounder. And, oh yes, the invisible glockenspiel of Princess Schmakenspiel, the—"

"Och! I've heard enough!" Wizzencoots exclaimed. "I've been sailin' all me life, an' I've nae heard o' any o' that fiddle-faddle yeur clackin' yeur beak about. Now why dinnae yeu tell us what yeu really want, owl?"

Nitty Pitty blinked her golden eyes innocently and said, "Well, if you really think a quest is too much, there might be another way."

"I vote for the other way," Boomish said.

Nitty Pitty strode thoughtfully around her cave. "Yes," she drawled, "I think maybe there might be some other way after all."

"Well, if you could manage to tell us before sundown, that would be helpful," said Desdemona.

"Welllll," said Nitty Pitty, "it's a mere pittance really." She tapped her wing to her chin. "Winter is coming, you know, and we must be practical now, mustn't we?"

"I dinnae like where this is goin'," Wizzencoots muttered.

The owl swiveled her head and locked her sharp eyes on Wizzencoots's socks. Hungrily she stared at the red and green diamond pattern, the folded-over top seam, and the gold tassels hanging from the sides and hissed, "I'm cold."

"Ah knew it!" Wizzencoots barked, frantically pointing at the owl. "Look! She's fixin' her evil eyes on me beauties! ME BEAUTIES!" Hiding his socks with his paws, he scuttled away yelling, "Yeu listen teu me, yeu mottled sea hag. If yeu think yeu're goin' to lay a feather on me beauties, yeur two eggs shy of an omelet!" And with that, Wizzencoots sprinted into the lift and yanked frantically on the ropes. "Quick, Danny!" he cried. "Back teu the ship!"

Sighing, Dan went after him. "OK, OK, Gramps. Calm down."

Boomish watched, wide-eyed, as Desdemona stomped into the elevator where Dan was trying to pry the ropes out of Wizzencoots's paws. She glared up at the old dog, whispering some angry words Boomish couldn't quite hear. But Wizzencoots shook his head violently, the whites of his eyes showing. Finally, she threw up her paws and walked off the lift.

"Can't we give her something else?" Boomish asked, sneaking a glance at Nitty Pitty, her talons drumming on the floor as she waited.

Desdemona studied the owl, who stared levelly back at her. She shook her head. "It's the socks or nothing," she said.

"But then what are we going to do?" Boomish asked, looking from Desdemona's defeated face to Wizzencoots, who was still struggling with Dan, to the owl, who crossed her wings stubbornly.

"Master Boomish, it seems there is nothing we can do but head back to the ship and try to bake up a new plan," Desdemona said, unable to meet his eyes.

"But you said this was the only way to find the pan!" Boomish reminded her.

Desdemona looked up at him, hopelessness in her eyes. "I know what I said," she said quietly and walked toward the lift.

As Boomish watched her go, determination rose up in him. "Well you may be giving up," he said, "but I'm not. I made a promise to get back the pan and be everything the King of Desserts should be, and that's what I'm going to do!" He stomped determinedly past Desdemona, heading straight for Wizzencoots.

The old dog saw him coming and shouted, "I know what yeu're goin' teu say, so dinnae bother!"

Boomish stepped onto the platform, locked eyes with the old dog and said, "Wizzencoots, I need those socks."

"These beauties are mine, an they're stayin' mine," Wizzencoots snapped.

"But Wizzencoots," Boomish said, "they're just socks!"

Wizzencoots flinched like he'd been slapped in the face. "Just socks?" he gasped. "Why, these are genuine, Plush-Tufted Snugdowner Sheep argyle! There's not a finer article of snuggly footwear available in all o' the Bewhiskered Lands!"

"Oh," said Boomish, having no clue what Wizzencoots was talking about. "But—"

"I'm nae done!" the grizzled dog growled. "Once sheared an' spun, these treasures are triple stitched. Triple stitched! Dinnae yeu know what that means?"

"No, but—"

"It means that whatever foul wind or slushy sleet one may encounter, yeur feet, ankles an' shins will remain forever warm an' dry. These socks are nothing less than the physical embodiment o' divine woolen protection!"

"But, Wizzencoots!" Boomish said.

Wizzencoots clamped his paws over his ears and sang loudly, "La la la la!"

"Wizzencoots, listen," Boomish grunted, tugging at the dog's paws. "The other night—*unh*—you put your faith in me, and I saw us through," Boomish gasped, still wrestling with the surprisingly strong dog. "Now I'm asking you to—*unnh*! —put your faith in me again and give up your socks." Still fighting to cover his ears, Wizzencoots shot a venomous look at Nitty Pitty, who blinked innocently in return. "Please, Wizzencoots," Boomish said. "I've made a gigantuous mess of everything, and I'm trying to clean it all up! Won't you help me clean up?" Wizzencoots stopped struggling. Guiltily, he looked from Desdemona, to Dan, then back at Boomish, and slowly, he dropped his arms to his sides. "Please?" Boomish said.

"Och! Grousin' mulligrubs," said the old dog. He plodded over to Nitty Pitty Ulu and pulled off a sock. "There's Agnes," he said gruffly, holding it in his paw. "An' there's Josephine." He pulled off the other one and stood there for a moment, gently smoothing the red and green fabric and admiring the golden tassels as they glittered in the firelight. Finally, fighting back the tears, he said, "An' if I hear yeu've mistreated them I'll—"

Hooting triumphantly, Nitty Pitty Ulu snatched the socks and hopped around the cave, seaweed and feathers flying. Wizzencoots looked on, biting a paw in frustration. Excitedly, the owl pulled on the socks and stuck out her legs to admire them. Desdemona, who'd been checking her pocket watch, snapped it shut and cleared her throat, "Ahem!"

Nitty Pitty looked up. "Hmm? Oh, of course." Reluctantly tearing her eyes from her prizes, she hopped over to the cauldron, pulled a leather pouch from under her wing and sprinkled its contents into the pot. Using a piece of driftwood, she gave the mixture a good stir. Then she hopped around in a circle, first on one foot, then on the other, chanting to herself in garbled tones. Within a minute, a thick turquoise smoke spilled over the sides of the pot, and when it disappeared, Nitty Pitty waved Boomish over. "Here kitty, kitty, kitty," she said.

After a reassuring nod from Desdemona, Boomish cautiously padded over and peered into the cauldron. Inside was a shiny black surface, and as he watched, a scene appeared. A chubby Blackpaw stuffed into her pirate outfit shimmered before his eyes. "Hey," Boomish cried, his heart skipping a beat. "It's Nancy!" Then he scratched his head and his voice echoed as he said, "But why is she dressed like a pirate?"

Alarmed, Wizzencoots and Desdemona hurried over and looked in the pot as the scene expanded to reveal Blackpaw and some pirates standing in the Grand Kitchen of the Lemon

Meringue Islands. The pirates were prodding some confused Sweet Smiths with their swords while Blackpaw stuffed a pancake into her maw. In her other paw was the pan.

"No!" Desdemona shrieked, her face ashen.

"Oh," Boomish whispered.

Wizzencoots cursed, then said darkly, "Gentlemen, prepare yeurselves. This is no longer a rescue operation. It's a suicide mission!"

"Suicide mission?" Boomish blinked as he raised his head. "I know Nancy seems to have fallen in with a bad crowd, but really she's just the sweetest—"

"Och! Yeu daft hair ball," spat Wizzencoots. "Don't yeu see? Yeur pretty lass Nancy is Blackpaw!"

"Nancy is Blackpaw?" Boomish stuck his head back in the cauldron to have another look.

Across the room Dan's jaw dropped to the floor. "Boy, oh boy," he said. "I didn't know we'd be going up against Blackpaw when I signed up for this adventure. What are we supposed to do now?"

Desdemona dropped her paws. "I don't know if there's anything we can do," she said, a pained look on her face.

Nitty Pitty Ulu waved away the last wisps of smoke. "Well, what you do or don't do is none of my concern," she said, shooing them out. "Thanks for stopping by. It's been a pleasure doing business with you!"

Wizzencoots shot daggers at the owl as Desdemona pushed him toward the exit. "Yeu falsehearted, conniving, double-crossing, overgrown canary!" he sputtered. "Yeu took me beauties knowin' all along our mission was doomed. Doomed!" he yelled over his shoulder at the owl.

As Boomish and Dan followed Desdemona and Wizzencoots onto the platform, Boomish looked around at his friends' gloomy faces. "What?" he said. "So she'll steal some desserts and go back to her ship. Is that *really* so disastramous?" The others stared at him, their mouths agape. "What?" Boomish almost shrieked, looking from Desdemona to Wizzencoots to Dan.

"Master Boomish," Desdemona said, "all Blackpaw has ever wanted is to rule the Lemon Meringue Islands. Now she does. Do you really think she's going to take a few desserts and sail off into the sunset? Oh no! I'm afraid that from now on, desserts will be nothing but a distant memory in the Bewhiskered Lands."

"In other wards, yeu can kiss your cinnamon buns goodbye," Wizzencoots said.

"Oh," whispered Boomish as Dan untied the ropes, and the platform *eek! eek! eeked!* its way down the cliff face.

"Tut tut!" Nitty Pitty called after their disappearing heads. "Don't look so glum. After all, you never know. Miracles do happen!" After they were gone she added, "In fairy tales, anyway."

A Date with Destiny

None of the animals said a word as the lift inched its way to the bottom of the precipice in the fading light. Silently, they trudged down the trail to the boat, and as Dan rowed them back to the *Grizzella*, the only sounds were the splashing of the oars and Wizzencoots's occasional sniffle as he contemplated his bare legs.

Boomish kept glancing from Desdemona to Wizzencoots to Dan, his tail twitching agitatedly. Finally, as Dan secured the jolly boat and everyone climbed out onto the deck of the ship, he burst out, "So what are we going to do?"

Desdemona stared blankly at the cat. "Do?" she said. "Tell me, Master Boomish. Just what would you have us do? Take on Blackpaw and her band of pirates singlepawed?"

"Not *single*pawed," he said as he counted. "There are... one, two, three, four of us, and we each have two paws so that makes um—"

"Listen, laddie," Wizzencoots interrupted, grabbing Boomish by the shoulders. "It's basic math. We're talkin' loads and loads of pirates. Multitudes! It cannae be done!"

"Not to mention Blackpaw herself," Dan said. "No one goes up against Blackpaw...and survives."

"Well, I have to," Boomish exclaimed. "Don't you see? I did all this, and I have to fix it. Those islands were given to me, and I have to get them back. I have to make sure the animals of the Bewhiskered Lands get their desserts. And those poor little guys in the kitchen, whoever they are, I have to free them. It's up to me!" He searched their eyes one by one. Dan turned away. Wizzencoots shook his head.

Desdemona touched his arm and said softly, "Master Boomish, it's too late."

As the sun dipped further into the ocean, everyone was silent. There was nothing more to say. Except that Boomish said something anyway. "Too late, shmoo late. I'm going anyway. And maybe I'll fail, but I have to try." He walked to the side of the *Grizzella* and began tugging on the ropes to the jolly boat.

"Hold on there, laddie," said Wizzencoots sternly. "Just what do yeu think yeur doin' there?"

"What does it look like I'm doing?" answered Boomish, as the ropes became a knotted mess. "I'm leaving."

"But Boomish," said Dan, as he padded over and untangled the ropes, "you can't handle the jolly boat by yourself."

"OK, fine," Boomish said, his paws on his hips, "then I'll swim. Desdemona, check your maps and point me in the direction of the Lemon Meringues."

"Now, Master Boomish," Desdemona scolded, "this is quite unlike you. Please, you must stop all this talk of going on alone."

"I'm sorry, Desdemona," Boomish said, "but I can't." He strode across the deck to the chest of swords and started rummaging around. "Seems to me," he said as he pawed through the weapons, "that everyone's gone out of their way to help me out." Finding a sword to his liking, Boomish straightened up and pointed it at each of his friends. "Wizzencoots let us use his ship," he said. "Dan worked hard helping to sail it. Desdemona, you stood by me even after all my mistakes. And the judge, well, we all know what he's given to help me out."

"But, Master Boomish," said Desdemona, "we're your friends. That's what friends do."

"Exactly, Desdemona! You've all shown me what it means to be a real friend. And now I want to be a real friend to all of you. And not only to you, but to the Lemon Meringues and the entire Bewhiskered Lands, because that's what a real Master Sweet Smith would do."

Each lost in their own thoughts, no one said a thing as Boomish slid the sword through his belt and prepared to dive into the sea. "I'm sorry, everyone," he said. "But I can't stay here, safe on board the *Grizzella*, while everyone's in danger of losing everything. I have to be a friend."

For a moment, the only sounds were the sails flapping in the wind. Then Desdemona spoke. "Well," she said, "seeing as I was appointed to escort you back to the Lemon Meringues, I couldn't possibly let you go alone."

"Really, Desdemona?" Boomish said.

"If you're going, I'm going," she said.

Wizzencoots studied them for a moment and then said, "Och, I've lived a long life. Might as well go out with a bang!"

Dan frowned at his grandfather, but Wizzencoots stared back at him defiantly. Realizing the old dog wasn't going to change his mind, Dan said, "Well, it looks like we're going up against Blackpaw. I'm in."

Boomish looked around at his friends. "I—I'm really— thanks, guys," he said hoarsely.

"Well," said Desdemona, "now that that's settled, we'd best be off. If this wind keeps up, we can be at the islands by morning."

"Hoist the anchor, Danny," Wizzencoots cried. "We've got a scurvy stray teu teach some manners teu!"

The next morning, Boomish was awakened by Desdemona's excited voice. "Master Boomish, Dan, Wizzencoots. Wake up! We've reached the Lemon Meringues!"

Rubbing the sleep from his eyes, he climbed out of bed and up the dim stairway after Dan and Wizzencoots. As the trio trotted across the deck in the early morning light, Boomish could make out the gray outlines of several islands, the largest of which had a natural harbor surrounded by headlands on both sides. A fleet of trading ships was tied alongside the docks, and at the end of the longest pier floated a black three-masted brigantine, the *Cat O' Nine Tails*.

"There she is!" crowed Wizzencoots as he spotted Blackpaw's ship. "Noo, what's the plan?" he asked Desdemona, rubbing his paws together. "I know it'll be a doozie seein' as how yeu've got the lay of the land on those islands."

Desdemona handed the wheel over to Dan and looked up in surprise. "But, Wizzencoots," she said, "this is Master Boomish's quest. I'd never be so presumptuous as to plan the attack without his consent."

Everyone looked at Boomish. "Oh, right," Boomish said. "The plan! Well of course I've got a plan." He sidled over to the big dog and whispered behind his paw, "Hey, Dan, umm, you wouldn't happen to have—"

"Blasted barnacles," spat Wizzencoots, "I cannae believe it! We're five minutes from a battle with Blackpaw an' we've nae plan!"

Dan's eyes narrowed as he looked at the horizon. "Well," he said, "the sun's about to come up, and as much as I hate to say it, I think I'd better turn the ship around before we're spotted."

Desdemona was about to agree when Boomish picked up the spyglass and held it to his eye. "Wait!" he cried, holding up a paw as he scanned the harbor. "I've got an idea!"

The first thing he saw was the tree-lined beach of the bay. Scattered beneath the trees were groups of sleeping Marzipan Grenadiers. Their swords were stacked in a large pile, guarded by a sleeping pirate weasel. Swinging the scope to the right, he examined Blackpaw's ship. No one was on deck, and all seemed to be quiet. His tail twitching excitedly, Boomish lowered the scope and said, "The pirates are still asleep. And I think if we get there before anyone wakes up, we can free the

Grenadinos and then we'll have a fighting chance against the pirates!"

Dan gripped the wheel, waiting for the order to turn the ship around. "Well," Boomish said eagerly, "what do you think?"

Desdemona nodded slowly. "That just might work," she said.

Wizzencoots grabbed the spyglass from Boomish and peered through. "Well of course it'll wark!" he crowed, confirming Boomish's findings. "Everyone knows pirates dinnae wake until after sunup." Sweeping the scope to the top of a bluff, he zeroed in on the island's pan-shaped alarm gong. "Why," he said as he scanned, "as long as the sun stays where she is far three more minutes, we'll catch those scoundrels with their pants—" Wizzencoots paused as he spied a sleeping skunk resting against the bottom of the gong. The next second, a ray of sunlight peeked over the horizon, zoomed past the *Grizzella* and hit the skunk directly in the face. The pirate squinted, rubbed his eyes, picked up his own spyglass, and pointed it directly at Wizzencoots. "Och! I dinnae believe it," the old dog cursed. "Cannae we catch a break?"

For a second, the skunk and Wizzencoots stared at each other through their spyglasses. Then the pirate jumped up, grabbed the giant spatula, and whacked the pan. *Gong!* The sound was still reverberating across the island as the skunk dropped the spatula and waddled as fast as he could toward the *Cat O' Nine Tails*.

Desdemona ordered Dan to turn the ship around. "We've been spotted," she cried. "It's hopeless!"

Boomish slumped, his heart in his stomach, as Dan began to spin the wheel. But Wizzencoots said, "Nae. Hold her steady, Danny."

"Wizzencoots! What do you think you're doing?" Desdemona cried.

Wizzencoots waved her off as he tapped a paw to his chin and paced the deck. "Let's see, now..." he mumbled, "we've lost the element o' surprise, we're outnoombered...we've nae cannons..." Suddenly he froze. "Aye," he whispered, a crazy gleam in his eye. "Looks like it's time far plan B."

"What's plan B?" Boomish asked, while Desdemona stared at the fixated dog.

"Someone had better tell me what to do," Dan called as the *Grizzella* splashed toward the entrance to the bay. "I'm almost out of room!"

"Boomish, Danny," Wizzencoots barked as he stormed over to the wheel. "Hoist the main!"

"But, Gramps!" said Dan. "We won't be able to stop in time. We'll be going too fast."

Wizzencoots shoved Dan aside and grabbed the wheel. "That we will, Danny boy! That we will! Hee hee!"

Desdemona looked wide-eyed at the rapidly approaching harbor. "Wizzencoots, have you lost your mind?" she squeaked.

"Och, far cryin' in a rain barrel!" Wizzencoots cursed. "Will everyone stop all the fiddledeedee and hoist the main?"

Boomish and Dan ran to the main mast, their paws a blur as they pulled up the sail. Immediately, the *Grizzella* lurched forward and entered the harbor at full speed. As Boomish and Dan hurried back to the helm, Desdemona retrieved the swords and tossed a couple to Dan and Wizzencoots. Handing the last sword to Boomish, she said, "Whatever happens, I want you to know, I think you've turned out to be one of the best pumpkin pies ever baked."

Before Boomish could answer, she ran to the bow, pulling him along with her. The beach was awash with rays of sunlight, and Boomish could see the Marzipan Grenadiers, their ears perked, looking from the speeding *Grizzella* to the pirate ship. "Why are they just standing there?" Boomish asked. "Why don't they fight?"

"Without someone to guide them, they don't know what to do. They need a leader," Desdemona said, and she looked up at Boomish. "They need you." For the first time, Boomish was important. Not because of his title, but because he was needed. A warm and fuzzy feeling filled his heart.

Over on the *Cat O' Nine Tails*, the skunk was racing about, pointing out the oncoming *Grizzella* to the growing number of pirates emerging onto the deck. The pirates' mouths dropped open, and they scrambled to launch the ship and load their cannons. Boomish stood on tiptoes, searching for Blackpaw among the scrambling pirates, but she was nowhere to be seen.

Behind the wheel, Wizzencoots was a dog possessed. His eyes were bulging, and his fur looked like he'd been on the losing end of a fight with an electric eel. Flecks of slobber flew from his jowls as he shouted, "Now yeu've done it! Yeu've gone an made me bad crazy! Do yeu hear me, Blackpaw? I'm comin' far yeuuu!" He spun the wheel, and the bow of the

Grizzella came about until it pointed directly at the brigantine. Dan stood next to his grandfather, his fur and his tail as stiff as a board. "I've got yeu in my sights!" Wizzencoots cried. "There's nowhere to run! Doom is upon yeu! Howoo! How, how, HOWOO!!"

Catching the fever, Dan took up the cry. "Howoo HOWOO!!" Not wanting to be left out, Boomish bared his fangs, raised his claws, and hissed. Realizing the speeding *Grizzella* was about to ram the *Cat*, Desdemona hightailed it back to the main mast, grabbed a rope, and held on for dear life.

"Prepare far impact!" Wizzencoots boomed, clutching the wheel in a death grip. Boomish hugged Dan's leg as Dan braced himself against the railing in front of the wheel.

The next instant, the bow of the *Flying Grizzella* crashed into the hull of the *Cat O' Nine Tails* with a *smash*! Pieces of wood exploded into the air, and pirates rolled like barrels across the deck of the skewered ship.

Tossed onto the deck by the crash, Wizzencoots, Dan, and Boomish jumped up, drew their swords, and ran toward the enemy ship, passing Desdemona, who was pulling a long hairpin from her babushka. "Master Boomish, wait," the mouse cried, grabbing hold of his tail as it flew by. "The Grenadiers!"

Boomish glanced at the beach where the Marzipan Grenadiers were watching the commotion and whining. "Right," he said with a nod and changed course, racing to the side of the *Grizzella,* where it had plowed through the dock.

Desdemona watched him go, then raced after Dan and Wizzencoots who were jumping aboard the *Cat.* As Dan hit the deck of Blackpaw's ship, Boomish landed on the dock and ran as fast as he could toward the shore.

In less than a minute, Boomish reached the Grenadiers. They recognized him instantly as the Master Sweet Smith and gathered around him, wagging their stumpy tails. "Attention!" cried Cocoa, saluting Boomish with his paw. The rest of the Grenadiers stood at attention, waiting for Boomish to give his orders.

"Hi," Boomish said, gasping for air as he looked into their smiling eyes. "Sorry I can't talk right now, but we have to get your swords and help Desdemona defeat the pirates."

Cocoa nodded and cried, "Allez! Allez! Forward march!" With Boomish in the lead, the dogs began double-quickstep marching through the sand toward their weapons.

Seeing them coming, the pirate weasel hopped nervously from side to side, pointing his sword at them and snarling, "Come any closer and I'll run you all through!"

"All of us?" Boomish said, glancing at the marching dogs. "Not likely."

Being the weasel that he was, the pirate dropped his sword. "Just kidding," he said, and ran off.

Immediately, the Grenadiers armed themselves, and Boomish called out, "Come on, troops. Let's go get Blackpaw!"

The Grenadiers formed ranks and began marching up the trail leading to the kitchen. "Wait!" Boomish cried. "Where are you going? The pirates are that way." He pointed to the *Cat*.

Mocha shook his head. "But Blackpaw, she is zat way," he said, nodding at the trail.

Boomish realized the reason he hadn't seen Blackpaw on the pirate ship was because she wasn't there. He danced in place for a moment, looking from the ship to the island. Finally, he said, "You guys go help Desdemona. I'm going after Blackpaw." Cocoa saluted and quickly led the Grenadiers toward the pier while Boomish took off up the trail.

Meanwhile, the Flying Grizzellers were holding their own against the disorganized pirates. Dan used his sword to disarm five pirates at a time. Wizzencoots was right behind him, confusing them with his jig-like footwork. Desdemona backed Jeremiah into a corner, expertly maneuvered her hairpin past his sword, and poked him in the belly. Dropping his sword, Jeremiah screamed in pain and cried, "Ooo ooo! I surrender, yes I do! Abandon ship! Run for your lives!"

Following the muskrat's orders, the pirates ran for the rails until the boatswain, who was good at math, turned around and counted the raiding party. "Hang on, mates," he cried in surprise. "There's only three of them!" The other pirates stopped running and after verifying there were indeed a lot more pirates than nonpirates, turned on the Flying Grizzellers, menacing snarls on their faces.

"This dinnae look good," Wizzencoots mumbled, bumping into Desdemona as they backed toward the stern.

"I agree," said Desdemona, her eyes darting from pirate to pirate. "What is keeping those Grenadiers?"

Dan swung his sword at a rat who was getting too close. "I don't know," he said, "but we're outnumbered twenty to one. If they don't get here soon, we don't stand a chance."

Just Desserts

Blackpaw's red velvet coverlet slid down over her well-fed belly as she sat up in her four-poster bed. Leaning back against her gold-trimmed pillows, she stretched a pair of sausage-shaped arms languidly over her head and yawned, exposing a rainbow of day-old candy stuck between her teeth. "Now, what shall we have for breakfast, hmm?" she asked herself as she looked around the Grand Kitchen, for that was where she was.

If the kitchen had needed a good scrubbing before Desdemona left on her mission, now it looked like a troop of monkeys had moved in and had a food fight every day since. The floors were hidden beneath a winter wonderland of flour and tables were slick with rivers of broken eggs. Layers of dried batter coated the walls and ceiling. The sink was overflowing with dirty dishes, used baking pans and spoons were strewn across the counters, and the rolling dessert racks crammed full of days old, disastrous desserts lay haphazardly around the room.

The Sweet Smiths sat chained together against the ovens on the far side of the room. They glared at Blackpaw as she considered them, drumming a brown-stained paw on her coverlet. "Hmm...those useless creatures can't seem to make anything right without a recipe, and I'm tired of pancakes," she pouted, glancing at the handle of the well-used pan sticking out from under a pillow. "I've got to get that book open! Now where is it?"

Impatiently, she rifled through her bedding, tossing candy wrappers and bits of crust onto the flour-covered floor until finally her paw bumped against the leather cover of the Master Book of Recipes. As she pulled it out, the Sweet Smiths muttered to one another. "That is not a Nice Lady!" whispered one.

"No! That's a *fat* lady!" said another. The rest of the Sweet Smiths nodded in agreement as Blackpaw gazed hungrily at the book.

"It's mine," she hissed. "All mine." Then, hugging the book to her food-encrusted shirt, Blackpaw cried out, "Look at me now, Mother! Every recipe for every dessert that was ever denied me is now in my paws! Now, if I could just get it open..."

Boomish stood before the front door of the Grand Kitchen, his heart pounding in his chest. "Crivvens," he whispered. "I'm about to take on the most villamous pirate in the Bewhiskered Lands. Hmm...Maybe I should've brought some of those Grenadinas with me." Hesitantly, he reached for the handle and was about to pull when he decided it might be a good idea to see just how many pirates were in there. Stealthily, he circled around the side of the building and peeked in a window.

Blackpaw was in bed talking to the Master Book of Recipes, and Boomish breathed a small sigh of relief. He didn't see any pirates, and surely the extra weight Blackpaw had put on would slow her down. Maybe he had a chance after all. Then he caught sight of the Sweet Smiths pulling dejectedly on their chains, and his eyes narrowed in anger. "Crivvens!" he exclaimed. "Those poor little guys! How could anyone be so despicamous?" Ducking down, he crept around the building to the back door. Slowly, he cracked it open and peeked inside.

The movement of the door caught the eye of one of the Smiths. He studied Boomish's furry face and his eyes brightened. "Hey," he chirped, nudging the Smith next to him. "Look at that guy!"

The other Smith looked over at Boomish and said with a grin, "Oo! I like that guy! He's a Nice Guy!" The two nodded vigorously and whispered to the others, who glanced at Boomish and instantly lit up.

"Hey, Nice Guy! Hi! Hi, Nice Guy!" they murmured, waving at Boomish, who stuck his paw through the crack and waved back. Wanting to be closer to the Nice Guy, the Smiths began moving en masse toward the back door, their chains clinking while Blackpaw spoke wheedlingly to the book, a desperate look in her eye.

"Now I know you want to open up for Captain Blackpaw," she said, licking her lips. "Maybe you just need to hear some special words, hmm?" She frowned while her stomach rumbled irritably. "How about, 'Oh, Bookie wookie, I do so want a cookie, so let me take a looky, and I'm sorry I played hooky'? Now open up!" she ordered, pulling with all her might. The cover still wouldn't budge, so Blackpaw threw off her blanket and used her hind legs to try to bunny kick the book open. "Unh!" she screamed, collapsing onto her back in defeat.

The Smiths, meanwhile, had left the back door and were moving in a tight huddle toward Blackpaw's bed. Winded from all the kicking, Blackpaw decided she needed more energy if she was going to get the book open. She was just pulling the pan out from under her pillows when a familiar voice said, "Something wrong, Nancy?" Blackpaw's eyes narrowed as she whipped around. A few paces away, the cluster of Sweet Smiths broke apart and out stepped Boomish, sword in paw. "Or should I say...Blackpaw?"

A nasty grin spread across Blackpaw's sticky face. "Well, well, well," she said. "If it isn't"—she batted her eyelashes and her voice turned high and sweet—"Boomish of Briarberry!"

Boomish flushed in embarrassment while Blackpaw awkwardly rolled out of bed, dropping the pan onto the floor in the process. Unfazed, she stomped on its handle, sending it flying into the air, and with her eyes locked on Boomish, caught it on its way down. "Lose something?" she taunted.

"Stolen is more like it," Boomish replied indignantly. "And I'm here to take it back."

"Well, if you want it," Blackpaw said sweetly, tossing the pan onto the bed, "come and get it!" she snapped.

Back on the *Cat O' Nine Tails*, Wizzencoots, Dan, and Desdemona stood with their backs against a mast, desperately blocking the blows Blackpaw's crew rained down on them. "I can't keep this up much longer," Desdemona panted. "There are just too many of them!"

Before she could utter another word, a possum wearing an eye patch swung his sword and knocked the hairpin from her paw. Grinning, he zeroed in for the kill when a loud howl made him jump. "Aroo!" The pirates spun around to see Grenadier after Grenadier climbing over the rails and dropping onto the deck of the ship.

"Thank Betsy," whispered Desdemona as the pirates scattered, some racing to meet the Grenadiers and others spreading out around the Grizzellers.

"Yeu're in far it noo, yeu scurvy sea scum!" Wizzencoots bellowed.

In the Grand Kitchen, the Sweet Smiths scurried out of the way as Boomish held out his sword, and like the gentleman he was becoming, waited for Blackpaw to retrieve hers. Blackpaw searched the filthy floor for her weapon and finally found it under the bed. She bent over to pick it up, but instead of saying, "En guard," she flew at Boomish, her sword aimed for his heart.

Just in time, Boomish lifted his blade, blocking the blow, and for a moment they were locked together, so close he could smell the maple syrup on her fur. "You know, Booboo," Blackpaw said with a snarl, "it would be far less painful to surrender now."

"I'll never surrender to *you*, Nancy," Boomish grunted, straining to hold his ground against the hefty cat.

"Blackpaw's the name, and don't you forget it," she said. She threw Boomish back and lunged, her sword pointed at his belly. Boomish spun to the left, and the Sweet Smiths gasped as Blackpaw's blade missed him by a hair.

"Crivvens!" Boomish gasped. "For a big girl, you move pretty quick." Blackpaw froze, a stunned look on her face. She looked down at her bulky belly, gave it a poke, and stared in disbelief as its blubbery surface rippled like rings on a pond. Screaming with outrage, she ran at Boomish, her sword swiping at him again and again.

Barely managing to block the onslaught of blows, Boomish retreated behind a rolling dessert rack. Breathing heavily, Blackpaw tried to flush him out with her sword. As the Sweet Smiths cheered him on, Boomish ducked from one side of the rack to the other each time Blackpaw took a stab at him. Tiring of the game and tiring in general, Blackpaw shoved the rack out of the way. It rolled across the room, leaving Boomish exposed. Wiping the sweat from her brow, Blackpaw wheezed, "Not—*huh*—too—*huh*—shabby for a big girl, eh, Booboo?" She raised her sword as Boomish searched wildly for a way to gain the advantage.

Swipe! went Blackpaw's sword.

Clang! Boomish's sword blocked the blow.

Swipe! *Clang*! *Swipe*! *Clang*!

Blackpaw huffed and puffed as she backed Boomish across the floor. Boomish took a quick glance behind him—he was running out of room—and as he did so, Blackpaw landed a blow to his arm. Yelping in pain, he dropped his weapon. Blackpaw kicked it away, sending it sliding under a baking table, out of reach. A cry of alarm rose up from the Sweet Smiths.

The she-cat blinked the sweat from her eyes and raised her sword for the final blow, but Boomish cried out desperately, "You know, Nancy, even if you defeat me, you're never going to be able to open that book."

"It's Blackpaw!" she snarled, a shadow of doubt crossing her face. "And what would you know about it?"

"I know that you're not supposed to be the next Queen of Desserts," he grimaced, holding his injured arm. "I know it, the little baking guys know it, and even that book knows it. And that's why it's never going to open for you." The Sweet Smiths murmured in agreement.

Blackpaw shot them a dirty look and snapped, "We'll see about that." Determined to prove everyone wrong, she strode over to the bed, her drumstick-shaped thighs rubbing together as she went. Throwing down her sword, she picked up the book, and using the handle of the pancake pan, tried to pry the covers apart. "Unh!" she exclaimed, straining with all her might, but the cover wouldn't budge.

Boomish was right. The book would never open for her. Once again desserts were denied her, and Blackpaw was outraged. "*No fair!*" she screamed, hurling the pan through the air. It landed on the floor with a *clang*. Blackpaw's syrup-stained face contorted in anger as she clutched the book in her paws. "I want my dessert!" she shouted, stamping her foot with each word. "My whole life it's been nothing but, 'No dessert for you, Nancy! No dessert for bad kittens!' Well no more! If I can't have my dessert, then guess what! No one will!"

Holding the book before her, Blackpaw stomped toward the ovens, a crazed look on her face. Boomish was wild-eyed. She was about to destroy the Master Book of Recipes. Frantically, he took a flying leap, landing just close enough to grab hold of one of her cankles. This slowed Blackpaw down to a shuffle, but she continued on, dragging Boomish behind her and muttering, "Not fair...Well, no more! None for me, none for you!"

Shortly after the Grenadiers swarmed onto the *Cat*, even the dimmest of the pirates could see they didn't stand a chance and surrendered.

While Dan and Wizzencoots helped the Grenadiers tie the pirates to the main mast, Desdemona was looking for Boomish. "Cream Puff," she said anxiously, "where is Master, um, I mean, the new Master Sweet Smith?"

"Oh!" Cream Puff said, his eyes lighting up. "He went to ze Grand Kitchen to fight ze white demon!"

Desdemona's eyes grew round with fear. "Wizzencoots, Dan, quick! We must help Master Boomish!"

Wizzencoots pointed to Cocoa and Mocha. "Yeu two, come with us. The rest o' yeu, stay here and guard this pile o' no good riffraff. That's right, I said it...*riffraff*!" Desdemona,

Wizzencoots and Dan leapt off the ship and ran up the path with Cocoa and Mocha quickstepping behind them.

Back in the Grand Kitchen, Blackpaw was ten paces from the ovens, still dragging Boomish after her when suddenly— *Thwak!* She froze for a second as raw egg dripped down the side of her arm. Glowering, she turned around and—*Thwak! Thwak!*—two more hit her in the face.

Seeing their Nice Guy in distress had infuriated the Sweet Smiths. Dragging their chain alongside, they had scuttled around the kitchen, raiding the icebox, the cupboards, and the dessert racks. After piling everything they could find on the baking tables, they launched their assault, and as Blackpaw wiped the egg off her face, the Smiths attacked in earnest. Eggs, flour bombs, puddings, and pies rained down on her, exploding in gooey splatters as they hit her furry body. "Bad lady! Bad lady!" they shouted as they threw.

Hissing and spitting in fury, Blackpaw held the book out, trying in vain to block the flying desserts. With the few extra seconds the Smiths' attack bought him, Boomish looked frantically around the kitchen for a way to stop Blackpaw. Suddenly, he let go of her leg and stumbled and slid across the goop-covered floor.

Squinting through the pie filling coating her face, Blackpaw continued toward her goal. The air was a blur with baked goods as the Smiths redoubled their efforts, but all too soon, the she-cat stood before an oven, the glow of its fire reflecting off the shiny goo dripping down her face.

The Smiths' paws dropped helplessly to their sides as Blackpaw raised the book above her head. As she gazed into the leaping flames, a tear ran down her cheek. "All I ever wanted was a piece of cake," she said hoarsely. "Was that too much to ask?" Her face contorted into a grimace of pain and anger, and as she gathered herself to throw the book into the fire— *Thunk*! Her eyes rolled back in her head, and she toppled to the ground, revealing a breathless Boomish standing behind her, the pan clutched in his paw.

"Sorry, Blackpaw," he panted. "No dessert for you!"

Just then, the big wooden door swung open, and into the kitchen burst Dan, Desdemona, Cocoa, Mocha and Wizzencoots, swords at the ready. Seeing Blackpaw lying in a heap on the floor, they skidded to a stop, their mouths agape.

Wizzencoots was the first to recover. "Now that is some sticky nastiness," he said, shaking his head at the mess that was Blackpaw. "But, far cryin' in a rain barrel, laddie. Couldnae yeu have saved a bit far me?" Boomish smiled.

The next morning, Dan and Wizzencoots knocked on the door of the Master Sweet Smith's cave. "Are yeu ready, laddie?" Wizzencoots called. "Yeur big moment has arrived." The door opened and the two dogs stepped back at the sight of Boomish dressed in the ceremonial garb of the Master Smith: gold chef's hat, red apron, and red cape trimmed with gold. In his paw was the magic pancake pan, shining brightly and humming happily.

"Wow," Dan said as Boomish stepped out into the sun.

"I couldnae said it better myself," Wizzencoots agreed. "Well, come on yeur highness. Dinnae keep the señorita waiting." He turned to go, but Boomish stopped him with a paw.

"You know what, Wizzencoots?" he said. "Just call me Boomish." Wizzencoots and Dan exchanged glances, and then followed Boomish down the trail to the orchard where Desdemona waited beneath the arching branches of a chocolate nut tree, the Master Book of Recipes in her paws.

As Boomish joined her, Wizzencoots and Dan fell back into the crowd of beaming Sweet Smiths and tail-wagging Marzipan Grenadiers. Everyone fell silent as Boomish held up the pan and placed his other paw on the Master Book of Recipes.

At Desdemona's signal, Boomish began the magic verse of the Lemon Meringue Islands: "With pan in paw and paw on book, I do swear to protect these cooks. Jelly roll, profiterole, brownie, and cake. With patience and kindness I'll help them bake." As the last word floated off into the air, the Master Book of Recipes trembled and opened. "Crivvens!" Boomish whispered.

The Sweet Smiths hopped into one another and cheered while the Grenadiers saluted their new leader. Desdemona wiped her eyes with a hankie, then offered it to Wizzencoots who blew his nose. "Blasted allergies," he said.

As the crowd dispersed, and Boomish headed off to the Grand Kitchen, a beaming Sweet Smith turned to his friend and said, "I knew I liked that guy!"

The End

ONE MORE THING

Sister Drusilla sighed happily as she looked around the dining hall of Dismal Manor. Now that Boomish was gone, her blood pressure was down and she was finally able to eat her meals in peace. She looked over at Sister Agnes, and the two exchanged contented smiles.

Sitting in his usual spot, Jack glanced at the empty space next to him while he listened halfheartedly to what had become the daily topic of conversation ever since his friend had left the orphanage. "I wonder where Boomish is now," Wesley said to nobody in particular.

"I don't know, but wherever it is I hope the food's terrible," Morris said as he glared at his soup.

"Come on, Morris, you can do it," chirped Francesca. "Only five more days to go."

The pig looked down at his belly. "I don't know," he said. "I'm wasting away to nothing!"

At the next table, Magnus stopped slurping his stew and turned around. "Well, maybe you should've picked a better friend," he said smugly. "Or is 'friend' too strong of a word?" Leaning over, he poked a paw into Jack's back and said, "Am I wrong, or have you still not heard a word from that mangy stray?" Junior snickered.

Jack glared at the two dogs. "Boom Boom will write. You'll see!" he cried. "He's just been busy. Right, guys?" he said, waiting for Wesley, Morris, and the squirrels to back him up. The others looked guiltily away.

"Busy scrubbing litter boxes somewhere I bet. Har har! Har har—"

Crash!

The entire room looked up as the double windows of the dining hall burst open and in flew the hulking form of Nitty Pitty Ulu.

"Heavens!" cried Sister Drusilla, shooting to her feet. "It's an invasion!" Sisters Gertrude and Mary Therese *baaed* in dismay.

Pushing up her spectacles as she scanned the room, the owl's yellow eyes lit up as she spotted Wesley. "Hoo *hoo*!" she cried and dive-bombed straight toward the dog. Petrified in fear, Wesley shut his eyes and prayed for a quick and painless death. *Plop*! "Happy belated birthday, compliments of the Lemon Meringue Islands!" cried Nitty Pitty as she climbed back into the air.

Wesley cracked open an eye and saw, sitting on the table, a large, brown-paper box tied with twine. He pulled on a loose end, and the orphans gasped as the box fell open to reveal an enormous chocolate birthday cake.

"Enough to share with your friends!" called the owl, shooting a warning look at the Sisters. "Now," she mumbled, "where is that—there he is! And isn't he a tasty looking morsel?"

"Eek!" Jack cried as the owl swooped down and scooped him up in a huge talon.

"What is the meaning of this?" demanded Sister Drusilla. "No orphans are allowed to fly without the proper paperwork! Come back here at once!"

The orphans stared in amazement as Nitty Pitty made a U-turn and swooped down on the head table. "Never mind!" cried the bear as she dove to the floor. At the last second the owl pulled up, dropping a scroll onto the bear's plate as she flew by.

In shock from the near miss, the sisters could only stare at the owl's disappearing tail feathers as she carried Jack out the windows and off into the evening sky. Once she was sure the owl was gone, Sister Drusilla unrolled the piece of parchment and read aloud. "Enclosed, please find all necessary paperwork for the adoption of Jack. Kindly forward all his belongings to Boomish K. Sullivan care of my address. Signed, *Judge Benjamin T. Oddkins.*"

ABOUT THE AUTHORS

Shared love of books brought Nick and Tara O'Riley together—they met while working at Borders Books and Music in Phoenix, Arizona. The two married in 1999 and welcomed their first child a year later. Two more children followed, and with them came endless amounts of reading out loud.

Maybe it was the lack of sleep, but at some point Tara began to believe she could create her own story, and during an early first draft, she asked Nick for some input which he gladly provided (he had quietly been waiting for an invitation). One version led to another, and another, and another, until they finally arrived at the story of Boomish.

Nick has a bachelor's in print journalism. Tara has a master's in educational psychology. This is the O'Rileys' first writing collaboration.

They live in Northern California, with their three children, two dogs, and a cat.

ABOUT THE ILLUSTRATOR

Matt Loveridge lives in the mountains of Utah with his lovely wife and children. He loves to hike, cook, play with his kids and draw, especially animals, and fun, silly things.

Made in the USA
Middletown, DE
05 June 2020

96772697R00109